A Science

The Magic School Bus®
CHAPTER BOOK
ROCKY ROAD TRIP

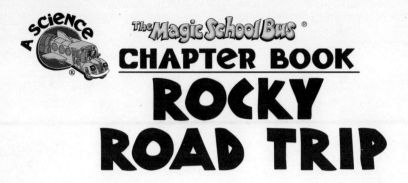

The Magic School Bus ®
CHAPTER BOOK
ROCKY ROAD TRIP

SCHOLASTIC INC.
New York   Toronto   London   Auckland   Sydney
Mexico City   New Delhi   Hong Kong   Buenos Aires

Written by Judith Bauer Stamper.

Illustrations by Hope Gangloff.

Based on *The Magic School Bus* books
written by Joanna Cole and illustrated by Bruce Degen.

The author and editor would like to thank Dr. John D. Humphrey
of the Colorado School of Mines for his expert
advice in reviewing this manuscript.

No part of this publication may be reproduced in whole or in part, or stored in a retrieval system, or transmitted in any form or by any means, electronic, mechanical, photocopying, recording, or otherwise, without written permission of the publisher. For information regarding permission, write to Scholastic Inc., Attention: Permissions Department, 557 Broadway, New York, NY 10012.

ISBN 0-439-56053-5

12 11 10 9 8 7 6 5 4 3 2 1   3/0   4/0   5/0   6/0   7/0

Designed by Peter Koblish

Printed in the U.S.A.   4 0

First printing, November 2003

.:INTRODUCTION.:.

Hi, my name is Carlos. I am one of the kids in Ms. Frizzle's class.

You've probably heard of Ms. Frizzle. (Sometimes we just call her the Friz.) She is a terrific teacher, but a little strange.

Ms. Frizzle loves science and will do anything to teach us about it. That's why the Magic School Bus comes in so handy. Believe me, it's not called *magic* for nothing. Once we climb on board, *anything* can happen. And it usually does!

We can tell when a Magic School Bus trip is coming up. How? We just look at what Ms. Frizzle is wearing.

One day, the Friz came into class wearing a dress with rocks all over it.

Since we were studying rocks and minerals, I didn't get suspicious right away. But it didn't take long to find out that a field trip was coming up. We were all in for a *grand* surprise when we found out where we were headed.

Let me tell you what happened when the Magic School Bus took us on a mystery trip to find hidden treasure!

CHAPTER 1

I staggered into Ms. Frizzle's classroom, carrying my science project in both hands. It was so heavy, I couldn't wait to set it down.

"Carlos," Tim called out. "You look like you're carrying a ton. What's in the box?"

"It's just . . . just my rock collection," I said, trying not to groan. "I found some big ones this weekend."

My muscles were starting to quiver. I had to put the box down soon, or I would have a rock slide on my hands!

THUD! I dropped the collection on top of my desk. A cloud of dust puffed out from the sides of the box.

"I guess if you want to rock, you've got to roll," Dorothy Ann said.

She and Tim laughed, but I just smiled and shrugged. Dorothy Ann — D.A. for short — and Tim know everything about science. They are neck and neck in every science contest we have in class. But this time, I was planning to outsmart them.

I lifted the lid and looked inside my rock collection box.

"Wait until you see my new pieces of sandstone," I said. "I got them from a cliff beside the Saddle River. It's a great spot for rock hounds."

"A great spot for rock heads?" Arnold said, looking confused.

"Not rock heads, Arnold, rock *hounds*," I explained. "You know, people who collect rocks and minerals."

Just then, Ms. Frizzle came into the room, carrying a box labeled SPECIMENS. She headed for the worktable by her desk. Then she turned over the box, and out tumbled a whole bunch of rocks and minerals.

Wanna Be a Rock Hound?
by Carlos

To make a rock collection, you first need to collect some rocks. Look in the school yard, along the banks of a stream, or in a park for rocks of different shapes and colors. Then arrange your specimens in a box or egg carton. Use a field guide to identify the rocks using texture, color, and hardness as clues. Label your collection, then put it on display.

I ran over to the table to see what was in Ms. Frizzle's rock pile. The rocks were pretty cool, but not as cool as my rock collection. I had been gathering rocks for months. Every year, Ms. Frizzle gives out a Rock Hound of the Year Award to the student with the best science project on rocks and minerals. I was determined to win — and I had a special mystery rock that I was sure could help me do it. The only problem was I didn't know how to identify it.

"Ms. Frizzle," I said, "I brought in my own rock collection. Everything is all organized and labeled."

"That rocks, Carlos," the Friz said with a wink. "Then you can help me sort through this pile."

"I can help, too," Tim quickly added. "I did my project on the three categories of rocks — igneous, sedimentary, and metamorphic."

Rock Solid!

by Tim

What are rocks made of? Other rocks! The amazing forces at work inside and outside planet Earth

---

continually form new rocks out of old ones. Wind, water, and ice can break up rocks into tiny pieces. Heat and pressure can squeeze, bake, press, or melt one kind of rock into another. Geologists are scientists who study rocks. They sort rocks into three categories — igneous, sedimentary, and metamorphic — according to the ways they were formed.

By now, the rest of the kids had gathered around the worktable. Ms. Frizzle picked up a chunk of rock from the top of the pile. It was black and shiny.

"Meet mystery rock number one," the Friz said. "Everyone check it out. Then try to guess what it is. Think fast," she added, "because this rock is cool."

I moved in closer to inspect the rock. It was sleek and glossy, almost like glass. I could tell from its texture what category it belonged to. I was just about to tell everyone . . . when Tim beat me to it!

"Mystery rock number one is an igneous rock," Tim said. "Right, Ms. Frizzle?"

Igneous Rock

Igneous rock is formed from the hot, liquid rock found deep in the earth's crust. When this molten rock is underground, it is called magma. When it is above ground, it is called lava.

Most igneous rock is very hard. Igneous rock that cools and hardens underground forms slowly and usually has a coarse texture and contains visible crystal grains. Igneous rock that forms above ground cools and hardens faster. It generally has small or even microscopic crystals. Some volcanic rocks cool and harden so quickly that crystals don't have time to form. Those rocks are smooth and glassy.

granite

"Good detective work, Tim," the Friz said.

"It's an igneous rock that formed above ground, right?" I said. "That's why it's so smooth." I wanted to show Ms. Frizzle that I knew just as much about rocks as Tim did.

"Right, Carlos," the Friz said with a smile. "This particular igneous rock is called obsidian. See its sharp edges? Native Americans used obsidian rock to make arrowheads."

"Cool!" Keesha said. She picked up a gray

rock from the table. It broke apart in her hands. "Oops," she said. "What kind of rock was that?"

"It looks like clay!" I said, glancing at Tim to see if he knew the answer, too. "I think it's a sedimentary rock, like sandstone."

Sedimentary Rock

Sedimentary rock is formed by erosion. Erosion is a process where forces such as wind, water, heating, freezing, and gravity break off and move fragments of rock. The rock fragments - along with sand, pebbles, shells, and plant matter - create layers of what is called sediment. Over time, the sediment hardens into sedimentary rock.

Because of the way they were formed, sedimentary rocks often have visible layers or ripplelike markings. They are generally softer than igneous or metamorphic rocks. Some

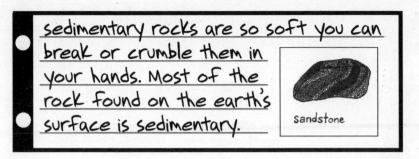

sedimentary rocks are so soft you can break or crumble them in your hands. Most of the rock found on the earth's surface is sedimentary.

sandstone

D.A. looked up from the pad where she had been taking notes. "According to my research, some sandstone is red because it has iron oxides in it."

"Is your hair red because of iron oxides, Ms. Frizzle?" Keesha asked.

"No, Keesha," Ms. Frizzle said with a grin. "My hair is red because my father's hair was red."

"That's called *hair*edity," I added. The class groaned.

Arnold was eyeing a polished white rock on the table. "Is this marble?" he asked, giving the rock a careful poke.

Tim leaned in to look at it. Before I could speak up, he said, "Good call, Arnold. It looks just like the marble sculptures in a museum."

9

"*Marble*ous!" Ms. Frizzle cried.

"Marble is a metamorphic rock," D.A. told us. "It's formed from a sedimentary rock called limestone."

Metamorphic Rock

Metamorphic rock forms when sedimentary, igneous, or other metamorphic rocks are squeezed and baked by pressure and heat below the earth's surface.

When heat and pressure together form a metamorphic rock, it has layers or bands of crystals that all point in the same direction. When heat alone forms a metamorphic rock, its crystals point in many directions and may not form layers or bands.

marble

D.A. and Tim knew everything about rocks! If this kept going, I would never get the

Rock Hound of the Year Award. I needed to learn more, fast, so I could identify my mystery rock. "Geologists don't just study rocks," I blurted. "They also study minerals."

"What's the difference?" Phoebe asked.

From the Desk of Ms. Frizzle

Rock or Mineral?

What is a mineral? A mineral is a collection of tiny crystals, which are all the same chemical material and all the same shape. There are many different kinds of minerals, each made of a different kind of crystal.

What is a rock? A rock is a collection of one or more different minerals. For example, granite is a rock made from magma that contains the minerals gray quartz, pink feldspar, and black mica.

"Color and texture aren't the only things to look for when you're studying rocks and minerals," Ms. Frizzle said. "There is also a way to test for hardness."

"We can use Mohs' scale," Wanda called out. "I'm doing my project on that."

Mohs' Scale #	Example Mineral	Other
1	talc	
2	gypsum	
2 1/2		fingernail
3	calcite	
3 1/2		penny
4	fluorite	
5	apatite	
5 1/2		glass
6	feldspar	
6 1/2		steel file
7	quartz	
8	topaz	
9	corundum	
10	diamond	

Wanda took out a poster she had made comparing the hardness of the ten different minerals on Mohs' scale. She had also included the hardness of some common things we knew, like a fingernail or a piece of glass.

"The higher the number a mineral has on the scale, the harder it is," Wanda explained. "See? Topaz has a number of eight. That means it can scratch anything with a lower number. But it can be scratched by a mineral with a higher number — like a diamond. Diamonds can scratch almost anything."

"Dazzling!" Ms. Frizzle said. "Here, Wanda, see if you can do a scratch test to identify which of these minerals is harder." The Friz handed Wanda two mystery specimens.

Wanda took the first mineral and scratched it with the second. A white powder fell on the table.

"This first mineral is definitely softer," Wanda said. "Even my fingernail can scratch it. I bet it's talc."

Wanda held the second mineral and

scratched at it with her fingernail. "This one is harder than my fingernail," she said, "so it's not gypsum." She took a penny from her pocket, then dug one edge of it into the mineral. The penny left a scratch.

"This might be calcite, number three on Mohs' scale," Wanda said. "Or, it could be another mineral that has a similar ranking."

"Wanda, that was Mohs-t brilliant!" the Friz said.

I couldn't believe that Wanda knew so much about rocks and minerals! Maybe she would be Rock Hound of the Year. I had to get the Friz's attention back . . . fast.

"Ms. Frizzle," I interrupted. "There's a rock I have that I can't identify. Could I show it to you?"

"There's nothing I love more than a mystery," the Friz said. "Where did you find this rock?"

I ran over to my rock collection and picked up the mystery rock. "I found it in our attic," I said. "My mom said it was my grandfather's. And he always called it the Bright Angel rock."

"Bright Angel?" Ms. Frizzle said. "That's interesting. Bright Angel is the name of a trail in the Grand Canyon."

I handed my Bright Angel rock to the Friz. She took one look at it, and her eyes got as round as saucers.

"What's going on, Ms. Frizzle?" Dorothy Ann said.

"Kids," the Friz said, "I've never found a rock like this before. But I'd like to find more like it! I think it's time for a field trip."

Ms. Frizzle had that special sparkle in her eye. "Come on, Ms. Frizzle," I begged. "What kind of rock do you think it is?"

But the Friz was too busy to answer me. She was already filling her backpack with rock hound tools.

"Follow me," Ms. Frizzle called as she took off out the door, with Liz right behind her. "We're headed for the Grand Canyon. And the Rock Hound *Rock*-et is waiting for us!"

CHAPTER 2

We ran out into the parking lot after Ms. Frizzle. She headed straight for the Magic School Bus.

"But I thought we were taking a rocket," I said.

"Just wait till we drive off . . . I mean, blast off," the Friz replied.

I scrambled into the Magic School Bus and sat right behind the driver's seat. The rest of the class climbed in after me.

Arnold looked even more nervous than usual. "Ms. Frizzle," he said, "don't rockets usually go out into space? I thought we were going to the Grand Canyon."

"Don't worry, Arnold," Ms. Frizzle said.

"This rocket isn't leaving the third rock from the sun."

"The third rock from the sun?" Arnold said nervously. "Where's that?"

"Arnold, we *live* on the third rock from the sun," D.A. said. "That's just another name for planet Earth."

The Friz revved up the Magic School Bus's engine. I noticed that it sounded different. And something strange was happening to our seats. Suddenly, we were leaning back, facing straight up toward the sky.

"Buckle up, kids," the Friz ordered. "Are you ready for countdown?"

"No!" Arnold yelled.

"Yes!" everyone else cheered.

"Okay," Ms. Frizzle said. "Since this is the Rock Hound Rocket, we'll count down with the Mohs' scale of hardness. Who remembers it?"

"I do!" Wanda and I yelled at exactly the same time.

"Let's hear it," the Friz said, punching buttons on the control panel.

Third Rock
by Dorothy Ann

Planet Earth is made out of four layers of rock. The outside layer – the one we stand on – is the crust. Earth's crust is hard and solid. It covers the planet like a shell. Below the crust is a much thicker layer called the mantle. The rock in the mantle is very, very hot and dense. Next comes the outer core, a layer so hot that the rock is melted. At the center of the earth is the inner core. The rock in the inner core is squeezed so hard that it's solid.

Inside the Earth

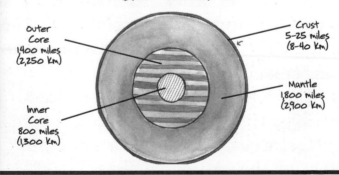

outer
Core
1,400 miles
(2,250 km)

Inner
Core
800 miles
(1,300 km)

Crust
5–25 miles
(8–40 km)

Mantle
1,800 miles
(2,900 km)

"Ten . . . diamond," Wanda and I started the countdown.

"Nine . . . corundum."

"Eight . . . topaz."

"Seven . . . quartz."

"Six . . . feldspar."

"Five . . . apatite."

"Four . . . fluorite."

"Three . . . calcite."

"Two . . . gypsum."

"One . . . talc!"

"Blastoff!" Ms. Frizzle yelled, pulling down a red lever on the control panel.

Suddenly, the Rock Hound Rocket started to shake. We all grabbed hold of our seats. Then there was a loud roar. Seconds later, the Rock Hound Rocket blasted off, straight into the sky!

I looked out the window. Good-bye, school. Good-bye, Walkerville. Everything kept getting smaller beneath us.

The Friz fiddled with some dials. The Rock Hound Rocket made a 90-degree turn and zoomed straight toward the west.

"Grand Canyon, here we come," I yelled.

"I don't care where we're going," Arnold moaned. "As long as I end up on rock-solid Earth!"

"Ms. Frizzle, why is it called the Grand Canyon?" Phoebe asked. "Is it the grandest canyon of all?"

"I know the answer to that," Keesha said. "I did my science report on the Grand Canyon."

A Great, Big Grand Canyon
by Keesha

Why is it called the Grand Canyon? Because "grand" means big, and the Grand Canyon is the biggest canyon on Earth. How big is it?

Width: At its widest point, the canyon is 18 miles (29 km) wide.

Length: The canyon is 277 miles (446 km) long from end to end.

Depth: The canyon is 1 mile (1.6 km) deep from top to bottom.

I was watching out the window to see if we were coming to the canyon. I wanted to be the first to see it. I couldn't wait to spot a clue that would help me identify my mystery rock.

The Rock Hound Rocket was zooming over a desert. I saw some amazing rock formations down below, but then I saw something that blew my mind away. We were coming up on a big hole in the ground! It was so huge, I couldn't even see the end of it.

"Wow!" I yelled. "That's a whole lot of hole!"

Everybody leaned over to look out the window.

"It looks like a big crack in the earth," Wanda said.

"That's not a crack or a hole," D.A. informed us. "It's the Grand Canyon!"

"Ms. Frizzle," Arnold said in a shaky voice, "we all might crack up if you don't do something about this crazy rocket. It looks like we're headed straight into the canyon!"

"Whoops," Ms. Frizzle said, taking a look

at where the Rock Hound Rocket was headed. "You're right, Arnold. We're headed to rock bottom!"

But the Friz didn't seem worried. She just grinned and punched a button on the control panel.

I looked out the window and saw the Grand Canyon coming closer and closer. What did the Friz have up her sleeve?

We were about to find out. The Rock Hound Rocket started to shake. Just as we were zooming into the canyon, the rocket turned into a helicopter — the Magic School Helicopter. We almost lost our stomachs as the helicopter came to a stop and then hovered in the air.

We had just caught our breath when Ms. Frizzle hit the gas and we took off again. The Magic School Helicopter buzzed through the Grand Canyon like a big insect. First we cruised along the South Rim. Then we buzzed over to the North Rim. Tourists standing along the edge of the canyon waved to us.

"The walls of the canyon look like a rainbow," Ralphie said. "Why do the rocks have all those stripes of color?"

We all crowded around the helicopter's windows to look at the canyon layers. The Friz kept dropping us down deeper and deeper into the canyon. The colors were amazing! We saw layers that were rusty red, creamy white, purple-gray, green, dark brown, and tan. Tim

even spotted some inky black rocks on the canyon floor.

From the Desk of Ms. Frizzle

History Written in Stone

From top to bottom, the Grand Canyon shows its history in twelve layers. Each colorful band of rock was formed during a different period in time. Some of the rock at the bottom of the canyon is over two billion years old! The youngest rock — the top layer — was formed 265 million years ago.

The layers in the canyon contain several different kinds of rocks, including limestone, sandstone, mudstone, shale, mica, quartz, and dolomite. The layers come in many colors, including rusty red, creamy white, purple-gray, green-gray, dark brown, and light tan.

Marita explained. "But my father's family has lived in Arizona for a long time. The Chees are Native Americans. Later, I'll show you where my ancestors lived."

I wanted to show Marita my Bright Angel rock, but Ms. Frizzle had other plans.

"Okay, kids," the Friz said. "It's time to saddle up!"

"Uh, Ms. Frizzle," Arnold said, "we aren't going to ride into the canyon, are we? No way am I doing that."

"Come on, Arnold," I said, "don't be stubborn as a mule. Climb on!"

Arnold just looked at me and shook his head. No one likes my jokes as much as I do. Well, I was more than willing to take the reins. I put my foot in a stirrup and swung up onto the mule. Suddenly, I had a perfect view of the canyon in front of us. It looked like a bottomless pit! A deep, dark, bottomless pit.

"Uh . . . do these mules know what they're doing?" I asked Marita.

"Not one of them has lost its balance yet," Marita said with a twinkle in her eyes.

Giddyap, Mule!

The mules of the Grand Canyon are trained to carry tourists from the top of the canyon rim down to the bottom. They are surefooted animals that carefully pick their way along the narrow ledges of the canyon.

"I'm not so sure about this," Arnold said as our mule train started down the canyon.

Part of me agreed with him. The path was steep!

Marita led the way on her mule. I was next in line behind her. Arnold and Ms. Frizzle brought up the rear.

I looked around and felt like I was in rock hound paradise. The Bright Angel Trail zigzagged down the canyon. Sometimes we rode through tunnels in the rock. Sometimes the mules had to pick their way around big

stone formations. Sometimes the trail was so narrow that our mules barely fit on it!

Then Marita brought her mule to a stop. All the other mules stopped, too.

"Look at the canyon wall beside you," she said. "Then run your hand across it. What do you see and feel?"

I took a close look at the grayish-white wall. I knew it was sedimentary rock because I could see how it had formed in layers. The rock had all kinds of things in it.

"I see a shell," D.A. said.

"There's a fish bone," Ralphie added.

"I see a trilobite," I said proudly.

"Does it bite?" Arnold asked nervously.

"A trilobite can't hurt you," I said. "It's been dead for a long time!"

"That's true, Carlos," Ms. Frizzle said. "Hundreds of millions of years ago, when this land was covered in water, insectlike sea creatures called trilobites ruled the earth. There's nothing left of them now but their fossils. And they're not the only creatures that left a rocky record in sedimentary stone!"

From the Desk of Ms. Frizzle

Set in Stone

Rocks have never been alive, but they can hold the remains of plants or animals that once lived. These remains are called fossils. Here are some examples:

mammoth footprint

petrified tree trunk

insect trapped in amber

fish skeleton

trilobite

If you find a fossil in a rock, the rock is probably sedimentary.

"There are a lot more fossils deeper in the canyon," Marita said. Then she kicked her heels against her mule's sides. "Giddyap," she said to her mule. Seconds later, we were all on our way down the canyon again.

The temperature was getting hotter and hotter as we rode deeper and deeper into the canyon. The only sounds we could hear were the calls of birds and the rush of the Colorado River below us.

Marita told us the story of the canyon as we went down. She described how wind and water had carved away the rock over millions and millions of years.

"This ride has seemed like a million years already," Arnold said, wiping the sweat off his brow.

As we neared the river at the bottom, we heard a strange rumble echo through the canyon. Marita stopped the mule train and looked up at the sky. We all looked up, too.

A flash of lightning zigzagged across the sky. Big, dark clouds covered the sun. Thunder roared through the canyon again. The rain started falling so fast that my shirt was soaked in seconds.

"Ms. Frizzle," Marita called out. "We have to get out of here! A flash flood could happen at any minute!"

From Marita's Grand Canyon Guidebook

Flash Flood!

In 1966, 14 inches (36 cm) of rain fell into the Grand Canyon in less than 36 hours. Where did all the water go?

It rushed down the main canyon and into side canyons as a 40-foot-high (12m) wall of mud and water. It tossed huge boulders into the river. It tore out trees like weeds.

In canyon country, heavy rains mean flash floods. Get out before it's too late!

The Friz wasted no time. She whipped a remote control out of her pocket. She aimed it at the top of the Bright Angel Trail where we had begun our ride. We watched as she pushed a red button.

In a minute, we heard a *chop-chop-chop* sound echo in the canyon.

"It's the copter," D.A. said.

We all looked up. The Magic School Helicopter was zooming down the canyon to our rescue. It landed on the trail right behind Ms. Frizzle.

"Get off your mules," Marita yelled. "We've got to get out of here! The mules can run up the trail easier without carrying us."

Arnold slid off his mule, and it took off like crazy up the canyon trail. The rest of our mules followed it.

Just then we heard a terrible roar coming down the canyon from the northeast.

"What is that sound?" I asked Marita.

Marita's face had turned pale. "Flash flood!"

⬤•CHAPTER 4•••

"What do we do?" Ralphie shouted. "There's no way we can fly out of here in this storm!"

I looked at Ms. Frizzle. She had to do something! And she did! She pointed her remote control at the Magic School Helicopter and pressed a red button.

Seconds later, the copter magically turned into a huge yellow river raft.

"Climb into the raft," Marita screamed, trying to make herself heard over the roar of the rushing water. "And put on your life jackets!"

We scrambled into that raft faster than

the mules took off up Bright Angel Trail. And not a second too soon!

The roar of the water coming down the canyon was getting louder and louder. Then, in a flash, it shot around a bend of the canyon—straight at us!

"Hang on!" Ms. Frizzle called. "Here it comes!"

One second we were on the canyon ledge. The next second we were zooming down the canyon on the top of a crest of water.

"Awesome!" I yelled. "This is one grand ride!"

Our big yellow Magic School Raft bounced up and down on the rushing water. The colorful walls of the canyon flashed by us.

"Help!" Arnold yelled. "I got water up my nose!"

"We're lucky we don't all have water up to our ears, Arnold," Marita said. "Just hang on tight, we're coming to some big rapids."

I was sitting at the front of the raft, so I was the first to see them. "White water!" I yelled.

A minute later, we were in the rapids. Everybody screamed at the same time. It was a wild ride!

Riding the Rapids
by Carlos

The rapids in the Grand Canyon are some of the most dangerous rapids in the world! A rapid is caused by a steep drop in a river's path that causes the water to run faster. When the water surges over rocks at this speed, it creates white water – a sure sign of danger!

Riding the rapids felt like riding a bucking bronco. I just had to make sure I didn't fall off!

The Magic School Raft bobbed up and down through the rapids. I turned around to see how everyone was doing. Arnold was green. The rest of the kids had eyes the size of saucers and were screaming. But Ms. Frizzle had a huge grin on her face.

"Hey, Carlos," she yelled. "How much fun is this?"

"It's a whole raft of fun!" I called back.

Everyone stopped screaming just long enough to groan at my joke.

Seriously, it was a rush. The flash flood carried us on down the canyon. Finally, the river widened and the water became calmer. At the same time, the rain stopped and the sun came out.

"Whew, I'm glad that's over," Marita said. "I checked the weather report before we left, and it didn't say anything about a storm. Usually, you get a little warning!"

"It's a good thing we had our Magic School Raft," Phoebe said. "I just wish we had a Magic School Kitchen. I'm starving."

"This Magic School Raft isn't magic for nothing," Ms. Frizzle said, opening a cooler strapped to the side of the raft. "Peanut butter sandwiches, coming up."

Peanut butter had never tasted so good. While we ate, Marita explained how the Colorado River created the Grand Canyon.

"It all started about 65 million years ago," she said. "Forces deep in the earth lifted up land to form the Colorado Plateau."

"I know what a plateau is," Phoebe said. "I wrote my report on it."

Flat as a Plate
by Phoebe

A plateau is an area of land that is flat on top and higher than the land around it. The word plateau comes from a French word meaning "little plate." But plateaus can be pretty big. The Colorado Plateau is 130,000 square miles (337,000 sq m)!

"For millions of years after the plateau was formed," Marita went on, "the Colorado River flowed across it. And that created a lot of waterpower."

"The river was so powerful," Ms. Frizzle continued, "that it carved a deep canyon through the rock layers that make up the plateau."

"And over time," Marita said, "it formed the Grand Canyon!"

From the Desk of Ms. Frizzle

Waterpower

How can water be so powerful? Gravity pulls water downhill toward sea level. As a river flows over sedimentary rock, bits of dirt, rock, and sand break off. The river carries the debris downstream, and the debris grinds down the rock it travels over. This process is called **erosion**.

That's how the Colorado River carved out the Grand Canyon. But erosion is slow — the process took millions of years!

"But how do you really know that the two sides of the canyon were ever together?" D.A. asked. "Maybe they were always separate."

"Geologists have found proof that they were once together," Marita explained. "And the proof is in the stone. If you look at one side of the canyon and then the other side, the layers match exactly!"

"Cool," I said. "Rock hounds are really smart!"

"You sound like a rock hound yourself, Carlos," Marita said.

I suddenly remembered my Bright Angel rock. I hoped I hadn't lost it in the rapids! I felt around in my pocket and pulled it out.

"This is part of my rock collection," I said proudly. "It belonged to my grandfather. And it's the reason we came out here. My mom always called it the Bright Angel rock."

"So that's why you wanted to go down the Bright Angel Trail," Marita said with a smile. "But there's no rock like that in the Grand Canyon. If there were, all the tourists would be digging for it!"

"What do you mean?" I asked.

"To find your rock, we have to visit a

mine . . . and I think I know just the place. My ancestors worked there . . . and it has a special name."

"What's it called?" I asked, beginning to get excited.

"The Bright Angel Mine," Marita said.

░CHAPTER 5░░

An hour later, we were speeding across the desert in the big yellow Magic School Jeep. The sides of the jeep were open, and we could see everything around us.

"Jeepers," I said. "This is one cool way to get around."

"Carlos," D.A. said. "Your jokes make you sound like a rock head, not a rock hound."

"Hey, look," Tim yelled. "What's that animal?"

We all turned to look at what Tim was pointing to. It was an animal that looked like a cross between a fox and a wolf.

"It's a coyote," D.A. said. "Like Wile E. Coyote in the cartoons."

"And look ahead," Marita said. "There's a roadrunner."

We all laughed at the funny bird speeding along on its long legs.

"How far is it to the Bright Angel Mine?" I asked, eager to find out where my rock came from.

"We won't be there for a few hours," Marita said. "But there are plenty of interesting rocks to see along the way."

"Like those?" Ralphie asked, pointing to some big red rocks sticking up out of the flat desert. "What are they?"

"I know, I know," Keesha said. "I wrote a report on buttes and mesas."

"Very good, Keesha," Ms. Frizzle said. "When we get back to school, maybe you can make some buttes and mesas out of clay."

"I could try, but they won't be as beautiful as Mother Nature's," Keesha said.

She was probably right about that.

Tables and Towers
by Keesha

The desert is dotted with strange, flat-topped mounds and hills. What are they?

A mesa is a flat-topped landform with steep sides. It looks like a huge table.

A butte is a small mesa that looks like a tower.

Mesas and buttes were once part of a larger, higher piece of rock called a plateau. Over time, wind and water eroded, or wore away, the rock. Mesas and buttes are what's left. In millions of years, they may be gone, too.

Mesa   Buttes

The desert was full of amazing colors and shapes. There were red rock arches and tall rocks sculpted by the wind and water into all kinds of shapes.

"I'm doing my report on geodes," Dorothy Ann said. "Do you think we could find any out here?"

"Ms. Frizzle," Marita said, "when we get beyond that big butte up ahead, turn to the left. There's a place where my uncle used to take me geode hunting as a kid."

A few minutes later, the jeep pulled up to a spot behind the big butte. We all followed Marita as she jumped out of the jeep and headed to a big rock surrounded by what looked like rubble.

"I don't see any geodes," Ralphie said, picking up a brown, round rock. "These are just plain old rocks."

Marita took the rock from his hands and examined it.

"What do you think, D.A.?" she asked.

D.A. pulled a rock hound hammer from her knapsack. She put the rock down on a flat piece of stone and hit it hard with the hammer.

"Gee, a geode!" Ralphie yelled.

D.A. picked up both halves of her geode. Inside were circles of different colored crystals.

"That one is a beauty," Marita said. "See what else you can find, kids."

While we all went geode hunting, D.A. shared her report.

We put our crystal balls into our knapsacks and climbed back into the jeep.

Crystal Balls
by D.A.

How do geodes grow? Here's how these crystal balls are created:

1. Gas bubbles are trapped inside layers of rock. They form holes, or cavities, inside the rock. Water seeps inside the cavities.

2. The water evaporates and layers of minerals are left behind. They form on the walls of the cavity.

3. Layer after layer of minerals build up. Each layer may be a different mineral and a different color.

4. When a geode is cracked open, it reveals the beautiful secret inside.

"Where are we going next?" I asked. "To Bright Angel Mine?"

"You'll have to be patient a little while longer, Carlos," Ms. Frizzle said. "There's something else we have to see."

"But you'll enjoy our next stop," Marita said. "It's petrifying!"

"Petrifying?" we all shouted together.

"I don't want to be petrified," Arnold said. "I was scared enough on that mule. And then there was the crazy raft ride. Can't we just go home?"

"Don't worry, Arnold," Ms. Frizzle said. "You won't get petrified. It takes millions of years."

We had no idea what the Friz was talking about. But we soon found out.

We came upon huge fallen trees that stretched out across the sand. The Friz stopped the jeep for us to get out and take a closer look.

"Hey, these aren't real trees," Tim said. "They're hard as rocks."

"They used to be trees," Ms. Frizzle explained. "But now they're stone. They're called petrified wood. It's a kind of fossil."

"Oh," Arnold said with relief. "That's not too scary."

From the Desk of Ms. Frizzle

How Petrifying!

Did petrified trees turn to stone because they were scared to death? No way!

Here's how it happens. Water that is full of a mineral called silica seeps into the tissue of a tree. The water evaporates, leaving behind the mineral. Over time, the tree's tissue is replaced by stone. That's called petrification.

The Petrified Forest in Arizona has a petrified tree that is 220 feet (67 meters) long by 10 feet (3 meters) in diameter.

"*Now* can we go to Bright Angel Mine?" I asked.

Ms. Frizzle and Marita looked at each other. A twinkle came into the Friz's eyes.

"Who wants to see where early Native Americans lived?" she asked. "We can get there fast in the Magic School Jet."

"Let's take off," Tim said. Everybody cheered.

No sooner had we all piled back into the Magic School Jeep than it turned into a plane and taxied across the desert.

Minutes later, we were soaring above the buttes and mesas. They looked like little clay sculptures below us. The plane zoomed along until, suddenly, we saw something amazing below us. There was a whole city built out of rock!

"Is that Mesa Verde?" D.A. asked in an excited voice.

"Yes," Marita said with a proud smile on her face. "Wait until you see the amazing homes the Anasazi people built into the cliffs."

The Friz buzzed the plane close to the cliff dwelling built by the Anasazi. Marita told us the story of the people who had lived there.

From Marita's Notebooks

Cliff Dwellers

The ancient Anasazi people built homes into the high cliffs of the Southwest. At Mesa Verde, the largest of the dwellings, called Cliff House, has over 200 rooms! Archaeologists believe that the cliff dwellings were built between A.D. 450–1300. Now Mesa Verde is a national park that you can explore.

"Now can we go to Bright Angel Mine?" I asked. "I'm itching to find out more about my rock."

"I think it's time to visit my uncle Mica," Marita said. "He can take us there. Ms. Frizzle, we're heading back west."

The Friz lifted the plane higher up into the sky. Soon we were winging our way across the desert.

CHAPTER 6

The Magic School Jet taxied to a stop in the desert. Marita was the first one off the plane. She looked really excited.

"Hurry up, kids," she said. "The trading post closes soon. I don't want to miss my uncle."

Up ahead, I saw an awesome-looking building. The sign above its door read TURQUOISE TRAIL TRADING POST. The place looked right out of a Western movie!

"Where is your rock, Carlos?" Ms. Frizzle asked. "I'll bet Mr. Chee can identify it."

"I've got it right here," I said, patting

my knapsack. "Do you think it might be turquoise?"

"No, Carlos," the Friz said. "I think you might have an even bigger surprise than turquoise."

I was getting more and more curious about my lumpy, yellowish rock. What kind of mine was the Bright Angel Mine?

As we walked up the wooden steps of the trading post, a tall man with gray hair walked out to meet us.

"Marita," he called out. "Who did you bring to visit me?"

Marita introduced us to her uncle, Mica Chee.

"Come on inside," Mr. Chee said.

We followed Mr. Chee into the trading post. The most amazing things were on the walls: Navajo blankets, buffalo heads, jewelry, and arrowheads and flints.

"I'm working on some gemstones," Mr. Chee told us. "I can show you some beauties."

"Is a gemstone a rock?" Phoebe asked.

"I know the answer to that," D.A. broke in.

What a Gem!

by D.A.

Gemstones are a rare kind of mineral. They are beautiful and hard. People value them for their color, and wear them in jewelry.

- A diamond is usually clear with fiery lights.
- A ruby is red.
- A sapphire is blue.
- An emerald is green.
- An opal is milky white with blue, pink, and green highlights.

Gemstones are measured by weight in carats. Long ago, gems were weighed on a balance scale against a pile of carob beans. One carat is roughly the weight of one carob bean. And the word carat comes from the Greek word for carob bean, Keration.

"Uncle Mica," Marita said, "will you show the kids your workroom?" As we all followed Mr. Chee into a back room, Marita explained, "Uncle Mica is a famous Native American silversmith. Wait till you see his gems."

Mr. Chee took us into his workroom. Spread out on a table were semiprecious stones of every shape and color.

"That's a garnet," Keesha said. "My birthstone is a garnet."

I spotted an amazing blue stone. It was the color of a deep blue sky.

"Is this turquoise?" I asked Mr. Chee.

"No, it's an even more valuable stone called lapis lazuli," Mr. Chee said. "And do you know how to identify lapis?"

I shook my head. All of a sudden, I realized that I knew a lot about rocks, but not much about minerals!

"Here, I'll show you," Mr. Chee said, picking up the lapis lazuli stone. "One way to identify a mineral or gemstone is called the streak test. Just watch."

60

From Mica Chee's Notebooks

The Streak Test

You can't always judge a mineral by its color. Some minerals, like tourmaline, can be black, brown, pink, green, or blue. But there is one good way to use color for identification — the streak test. Here's how:

1. Use the rough back of a white ceramic tile.
2. Rub the mineral across the tile.
3. Check out the color of the streak.

The streak of color left on the tile can help you narrow down what the mineral may be. Here is a list of some minerals and the color of their streaks.

Mineral Name	Color of Streak
Tourmaline	white
Green malachite	green
Black hematite	cherry red
Gold	golden yellow
Lapis lazuli	light blue
Pyrite	greenish-black

Mr. Chee scratched the stone against the back of a white tile. Sure enough, it left a light blue streak.

We spent some time using the streak test on other gemstones. Then Mr. Chee showed us his crystal collection. It was out-of-sight! Ralphie had done a report on crystals.

"Excuse me, Mr. Chee," D.A. said. "What are these stones that you set in silver? They are really cool."

"Those are turquoise stones," Mr. Chee explained. "The blue-green color comes from the copper and traces of iron in the stone. Take a look at the different stones. The more iron there is, the greener the stone."

"Why is your trading post called 'The Turquoise Trail'?" Tim asked.

"Because I know where to find deposits of turquoise in the hills around here," Mr. Chee said. "It's a family secret."

"We won't tell!" all of us said at once.

Marita gave us a serious look. "Can we be sure our family secret will be safe?"

Cool Crystals

by Ralphie

   Mineral crystals are nature's gems. They have flat sides, or faces. You can identify a crystal by the shape of its faces.

   Pyrite, also known as fool's gold, is shaped like a cube. Its faces are square.

Pyrite

   Beryl, including emerald, has hexagonal, or six-sided, faces.

Beryl

"We'll be as silent as stone, won't we, kids?" Ms. Frizzle said.

"Okay, Uncle Mica," Marita said. "They'll keep your secret. Let's go!"

Mr. Chee smiled and headed to the door, motioning for us to follow.

"Where are we going?" Arnold asked nervously. "And how are we getting there?"

I don't know how the Friz did it, but when we went outside, she was waiting in front of the trading post. And she was sitting on top of the Magic School Stagecoach — drawn by four horses!

"Yippee!" I yelled. "Can I sit up top with you, Ms. Frizzle?"

Before she could say no, I jumped up onto the wooden seat in front of the stagecoach. The rest of the class, along with Mr. Chee and Marita, climbed into the big stagecoach.

"Giddyap!" Ms. Frizzle yelled at the horses.

And we were off! The horses tore across the desert, pulling the bouncing stagecoach behind them. From inside the stagecoach, I could hear Arnold's voice.

"I don't want to see any bandits!" Arnold was yelling. "Get me out of this thing!"

We drove across the desert for an hour. Finally, Mr. Chee stuck his head out of the stagecoach window. "When you see a big red butte standing close to a mesa, steer the horses to the right and rein 'em in."

Ten minutes later, Ms. Frizzle pulled the stagecoach up close to the butte. The horses came to a stop in a big cloud of dust.

"Grab your rock hound tools," Ms. Frizzle said. "You can help collect turquoise for Mr. Chee."

I opened my knapsack and checked my tools.

Soon we were all chipping and chiseling away at the rocks around us. Tim found a big chunk of turquoise that Mr. Chee said was worth hundreds of dollars.

"Mr. Chee, it's amazing to see your family's secret mine," I said. "Can I show you a specimen that's part of my family history?" I pulled my mystery rock from my pocket and

Tools of the Trade
by Carlos

Every real rock hound needs at least two pieces of equipment.

A geologist's hammer has a square head on one side for hammering into rock. The other side of the head has a chisel edge for splitting rocks.

A magnifying lens is used to identify mineral grains. It makes a mineral crystal the size of a pinpoint appear large enough to see.

held it out to him. "It came from my grandfather. We call it the Bright Angel rock."

Mr. Chee took the rock from my hands and turned it over and over. Then he pulled a tile from his pocket. "Why don't you try the streak test?"

I couldn't believe it! I don't know why I didn't think to do the streak test myself. I ran the Bright Angel rock across the back of the white tile, then held it up for everyone to see. D.A. gasped. Mr. Chee smiled. The streak was golden yellow!

My eyes got wide. "Does that mean it's . . ."

"It's time we headed off to the Bright Angel Mine," Mr. Chee said. "Are you ready to search for gold?"

Was I ever!

From the Desk of Ms. Frizzle

Good as Gold

How can you identify real gold? Here's what to look for:

- a hardness on the Mohs' scale of 2.5–3.0 (That means it's pretty soft.)
- a shiny, opaque surface
- a bright gold color
- a golden yellow streak left by streak test

CHAPTER 7

The Magic School Stagecoach tore across the tumbleweed-dotted desert. We followed Mr. Chee's directions down a lonely road that wound through small hills. Ms. Frizzle and I had both put on cowboy hats and bandannas to keep the dust out of our faces.

Suddenly, I saw something that made the hairs on the back of my neck stand up. "Ms. Frizzle, what is that?" I asked, pointing to a group of buildings huddled in a river valley not far away.

"I believe that's a ghost town, Carlos," Ms. Frizzle said. "And Bright Angel Mine must not be far away."

I leaned down to yell into the window of the stagecoach.

"We're heading for a ghost town," I called to everybody.

"Did somebody say ghosts?" Arnold asked.

I didn't hear what Arnold said next because Ms. Frizzle pulled back on the reins, and the horses whinnied as they came to a stop.

"Would you hold the horses, Marita?" Ms. Frizzle asked. "I want to take a picture."

A bunch of us jumped down from the stagecoach and posed for the Friz, but just as she snapped the photo, I heard a spooky wind travel through the ghost town. I wondered if any ghosts would show up on the film when we developed it! We all climbed back on the coach in a hurry. The horses took off running.

Soon we were riding down the main street of the ghost town. We passed an old hotel, a saloon, and lots of abandoned buildings with broken windows and shutters banging in the wind. All the buildings looked ready to fall down.

From the Desk of Ms. Frizzle

Ghost Towns

During the Arizona gold rush of the 1860s, towns sprang up near places where gold was found. The buildings were put together quickly with cheap materials. And when the gold ran out, miners left the towns as fast as they had come. Many ghost towns still stand, with empty streets and spooky buildings. Only a ghost would want to live there!

Mr. Chee stuck his head out of the stagecoach window behind us.

"Ms. Frizzle," he called out, "take the next road to the right that leads down to the river."

"You bet, pardner," Ms. Frizzle said with a tug on her cowboy hat. I was glad to leave that ghost of a town.

The stagecoach bumped down the road to an old wooden bridge over the river. Mr. Chee called out for us to stop before the bridge.

The Friz and I jumped off our seats and tied up the Magic School Horses.

"Follow me over here to that bend in the river," Mr. Chee said to us after everyone had piled out of the stagecoach. "We're going to pan for some gold."

"Why are we looking for gold in a river?" Ralphie asked. "I thought we were going to a gold mine."

"The old gold prospectors found lots of gold in the rivers," Mr. Chee explained. "When the softer rock around gold ore wears away, the gold gets carried by water into riverbeds. It settles down in the stones and sand at the bottom of the water. Here, I have a couple of pans with me. Who wants to try?"

How could we pass up that golden opportunity? D.A., Tim, Phoebe, and Wanda went first. Then Arnold, Ralphie, and Keesha were next. I panned last with Ms. Frizzle.

From Mica Chee's Notebook

Panning for Gold

Here's how to pan for gold:

1. Find a stream near an old gold mine.

2. Use a shallow pan and scoop up the sand and gravel at the bottom of the streambed.

3. Work the pan in a circular motion in the water. The lighter material will go toward the edges.

4. Look at the heavier material that goes to the center and bottom of the pan.

Do you see a shiny yellow grain, flake, or nugget? Do the streak test. If the streak is yellow, you've found real gold.

I scooped up four loads of sand and gravel from the bottom of the riverbed. But I didn't see a sparkle of gold.

"I guess things just aren't going to pan out for you, Carlos," D.A. said with a grin.

I brought up one last scoop of stones and sand. And that's when I saw it! A stone about the size of a marble caught the gleam of the sun.

"I've struck it rich!" I yelled. Everybody came running over to see what I had found.

Are You Fooling Me?
by Carlos

Many prospectors thought they had found gold. But they were wrong! Instead, they had found "fool's gold." That's a nickname for a mineral called pyrite. How do you tell pyrite from real gold? Use the streak test. If it's pyrite, the streak will be black.

Pyrite is good for something, though. For centuries, it was used to make fire. Strike pyrite against flint or iron, and watch the sparks fly!

Mr. Chee picked up the nugget and held it up to the sun. Then he pulled out a tile and did a streak test. "We want to be sure this isn't fool's gold," Mr. Chee said.

It turns out I wasn't a fool. . . . The streak was bright yellow!

"You've got the golden touch, Carlos," Mr. Chee told me. "I think we should head on out to Bright Angel Mine. We'll see what you can find there."

Mr. Chee climbed up on the front of the stagecoach to drive with Ms. Frizzle. I climbed inside to show all the kids my nugget.

Before long, the bouncing of the stage-coach stopped. We all jumped out to see where we were.

"'Bright Angel Mine!'" I read from the old wooden sign hanging over the mine entrance. "This is it!"

"I hope we find buried treasure," Tim said. "I did a report on that!"

"I believe your grandfather must have worked this mine," Mr. Chee said to me. "It's where he would have found that chunk of gold in your pocket. Now let's see if your luck holds out inside the mine!"

Buried Treasure

by Tim

Gold, silver, and platinum are called precious metals. They are rare, beautiful, and expensive. Precious metals can be found in two places:

- in deposits that fill cracks in the earth's crust
- mixed in with sand and gravel at the bottoms of streams

What is the most common use of a precious metal? Silver is used in photographic film. Silver crystals on the film react to light and capture an image. Get the picture?

At the entrance to the mine, we found an old mine car from the days of the Wild West! It was only big enough for two people — but that wasn't a problem. We were so distracted by the mine that we didn't keep an eye on Ms. Frizzle. When we turned around, we had a big surprise. The Magic School Stagecoach had turned into the Magic School Mine Car.

I ran up to the real mine car and grabbed a spot at the hand pump that made the car go. Ms. Frizzle hopped in beside me.

"Okay," Mr. Chee said as the rest of the kids jumped into the Magic School Mine Car. "Pump that handle, and we'll be inside the mine in no time."

Ms. Frizzle handed out hard hats with lights on the front of them. And we were off! Ms. Frizzle and I led the way, and soon we were zooming through the dark mine. Liz steered the Magic School Mine Car behind us.

"Turn into the tunnel on the left," Mr. Chee called out. "That's where the last gold was found in here."

We made a quick turn to the left and shot through the darkness until we came to the end of the tunnel.

"Okay, everybody out," Ms. Frizzle said. "Here are some hammers to chip out the ore. Start hammering!"

I grabbed a hammer and went over to the wall of stone where the tunnel ended. The light on my hard hat lit up the rock face. I thought I saw what looked like a streak of ore zigzagging through the rock. I hit at it as hard as I could with my hammer.

All around me the other kids were chipping away at the walls of the tunnel.

"Hey, Mr. Chee," I said as my hammer

chipped off a chunk of rock. "I think I may have found —"

Suddenly, my voice was drowned out by a deep rumbling sound. It echoed through the tunnel we had come through. Then the earth felt like it was moving beneath our feet!

"Earthquake!" Mr. Chee yelled out over the rumbling sound. "We've got to get out of here!"

I grabbed the chunk of rock that I had

chipped off and stuck it in my pocket as I ran for the Magic School Mine Car.

"Let's go, class," Ms. Frizzle said. "We haven't a minute to spare!" Ms. Frizzle pushed the red button on her remote control. After that, everything happened faster than a speeding bullet! The mine car turned into a Magic School Bullet Train. We piled in, and the train shot down the tunnel tracks toward the mine entrance. I looked behind us. Rock was crumbling down from the tunnel ceiling and covering the tracks.

"I see light at the end of the tunnel!" D.A. yelled. We shot out of the mine . . . and not a second too soon. There was a giant rumble as rock crashed down and blocked the entrance to Bright Angel Mine.

"Whew, that was a close one!" Ms. Frizzle said.

"Too close for comfort," Marita added. Then she turned to me. "And I'm sorry you didn't have a chance to find gold in Bright Angel Mine just like your grandfather, Carlos."

I felt in my pocket for the rock. Had I

lost it during the earthquake? No — it was still there! With a big smile, I pulled out my rock and held it up in the sunlight.

The sun glinted off the streaks of gold in my rock.

"Carlos," Mr. Chee said to me, "you're as good as gold!"

CHAPTER 8

"That's a magnificent mesa, Keesha," Ms. Frizzle said. "And a beautiful butte."

"Thanks, Ms. Frizzle, but it's not as cool as seeing the real thing," Keesha said.

We were back in the classroom, working on our rocks and minerals projects. Keesha was making a clay panorama of desert rocks. Dorothy Ann was putting the finishing touches on a huge poster about geodes. She had her geode from the desert displayed below it.

I walked over to see what Arnold was doing. He had a sponge cut into the shape of a bone. And he had it sitting in a pan with water and Epsom salts.

"What's that, Arnold?" I asked.

"It's my petrification project," Arnold said. "I was so petrified this whole field trip that I thought it would be nice to see something else petrified for a change."

Arnold explained that the bone-shaped sponge would absorb the minerals in the Epsom salts and then turn as hard as rock. The sponge would turn to stone, just like fossils do.

I headed back to my project, my super-duper rock collection. I had added my gold nugget and my chunk of veined gold from Bright Angel Mine. I was rearranging them one more time when Ms. Frizzle tapped me on the shoulder. When I turned around, Ms. Frizzle was holding something out to me — a T-shirt that read ROCK HOUND OF THE YEAR!

"Yes!" I yelled. "That rocks!"

I pulled the T-shirt over my head. Everyone in the class began to cheer and clap.

"Listen," I said, "I've added something else to my rock hound project."

"We're all ears, Carlos," Ms. Frizzle said.

I turned around and pressed the button on my boom box. The music blasted out, and I jumped up on my desk, holding my piece of gold from Bright Angel Mine.

"This is 'The Rock Hound Rock,'" I said, grinning, "written and sung by the Rock Hound of the Year!"

The class started to clap with me as I sang my song.

The Rock Hound Rock

Check out this rock.
It looks real old.

It might be pyrite.
It might be gold.

Look at its color.
Look at its glow.

Check out its hardness
According to Mohs'.

I did all the tests.
And now I know.

I'm a rocking rock hound
With GOLD to show!

The class cheered. And that was the end of my most awesome field trip ever on the Magic School Bus!

Rock Riddles

1. I'm an igneous rock. I'm black and shiny. I have sharp edges. What am I?
2. I'm a metamorphic rock. I'm used to create beautiful sculptures. What am I?
3. I'm a sedimentary rock. I am a layer of the Grand Canyon from 275 million years ago. What am I?
4. I'm the third rock from the sun. What am I?
5. I look like a plain round rock on the outside. Inside, I have layers of minerals and crystals. What am I?

[Answers: 1. obsidian 2. marble 3. sandstone 4. Earth 5. geode]

Mineral Mysteries

1. I have a hardness of 8 on the Mohs' scale. What am I?
2. I have hexagonal, six-sided, faces. I'm known for my beautiful green color. What am I?

88

3. I can be black, pink, blue, or green, but I always leave a white streak. What am I?
4. I leave a black streak. I have a cubic shape. What am I?
5. I'm a gemstone used in Native American jewelry. I am green or blue, but if I am blue, I am more valuable. What am I?

[Answers: 1. topaz 2. emerald 3. tourmaline 4. pyrite 5. turquoise]

Join my class on all of our Magic School Bus adventures!

Also by
ZILPHA KEATLEY SNYDER

THE
HEADLESS
CUPID

Zilpha Keatley Snyder

Illustrated by ALTON RAIBLE

ATHENEUM BOOKS *for* YOUNG READERS
NEW YORK LONDON TORONTO SYDNEY

For Larry again, and moreover

ATHENEUM BOOKS FOR YOUNG READERS
An imprint of Simon & Schuster Children's Publishing Division
1230 Avenue of the Americas, New York, NY 10020
Copyright © 1971 by Zilpha Keatley Snyder
Copyright renewed © 1999 by Zilpha Keatley Snyder
All rights reserved, including the right of reproduction in whole or in part in any form.
The text of this book is set in Eco 101.
Manufactured in the United States of America
First Atheneum Books for Young Readers paperback edition July 2009
10 9 8 7 6 5 4 3 2 1
CIP data for the hardcover edition of this book is available from the Library of Congress.
ISBN: 978-1-4169-9052-9

INTRODUCTION BY THE AUTHOR

The Headless Cupid sprang from a number of my own long-standing interests and enthusiasms. As a kid I was always intrigued by stories about old houses, about big families, and about ghosts—particularly ghosts who are not completely and disappointingly explained away at the end of the book.

But then, in the late 1960s, I became aware of the poltergeist phenomenon. I had read several news stories about poltergeists and about research on the subject. Poltergeists, I learned, had been studied all over the world. They were not the deadly, all-powerful evil spirits that Hollywood liked to portray. Poltergeists caused a noisy and slightly destructive series of events that usually seemed to occur in the home of an unhappy teenager. And then one day I met a teenager who was "into" studying everything even slightly "supernatural." She was obviously using her interest in such things to punish her parents. And suddenly I had my Amanda, and the beginning of the *Cupid* story.

David, from whose point of view the story is told, is loosely based on a boy in one of the fifth-grade classes I taught—a boy who seemed to have a great deal of responsibility for his younger siblings, and who treated everyone with an amazingly mature kindness and sense of fair play.

Amanda, the would-be witch in my story, is David's newly acquired stepsister. She is a twelve-year-old who is angry about her parents' divorce and even angrier about her mother's remarriage into a family with four younger children. Amanda is a dedicated supernaturalist, but only until something scary happens that is not one of her own productions. David's four-year-old brother, Blair, on the other hand, represents the innocent magic that some very young, and very sensitive, children seem to possess.

The Headless Cupid was a fun book to write and seems to be, according to the mail I receive from readers, a fun book to read. And Janie, the Stanley family's self-proclaimed genius, and Blair particularly will always be among my favorite characters.

Zilpha Keatley Snyder

Chapter One

DAVID OFTEN WONDERED ABOUT HOW HE HAPPENED TO BE SITTING THERE on the stair landing, within arm's reach of the headless cupid, at the very moment when his stepmother left Westerly House to bring Amanda home.

When Molly appeared at the foot of the stairs, David knew she was leaving because she had her shoes on and there was no paint on her hands and clothes. Molly, who at that time had been David's stepmother for about three weeks, was an artist, and around the house she dressed like an artist, very informally.

"Oh, there you are," she said to David. "I'm going now to pick up Amanda. Would you keep an eye on the kids while I'm gone? They were down by the swing a minute ago."

David said he would and Molly left, smiling back at him from the doorway. He sat a minute longer enjoying the deep silence of the big old house, empty now except for him. Even then, before anything happened, he felt there was something unusual about that spot on the landing. There was a central feeling about it, as if it were the heart of the old house. It was also a good vantage point, with a view of lots of doors and hallway, both upstairs and down.

David got up after a while and went outside and found his little brother and sisters. He pushed them in the swing until he got tired and then he took them all upstairs to the room that he shared with his brother, Blair. The kids got out some toys, and after they'd settled down, David took a book and stretched out on the window seat where he could see the driveway. He read some, but mostly he watched for Molly's car and wondered about the future—and Amanda.

Amanda, who was Molly's twelve-year-old daughter, had been staying with her own father since before Dad and Molly's wedding; but now she was coming to live with her mother and the Stanley family. Suddenly to get an older sister—David was still eleven—after so many years of being the oldest, would make anybody wonder about the future. And David had a strong feeling that Amanda might give a person more to wonder about than the average stepsister.

That feeling about Amanda came partly from a few specific clues, but mostly from a premonition. Premonitions ran in David's family—on his mother's side—and the one David had about Amanda was one of the strongest he'd ever had. What it felt like was a warning, a warning to expect some drastic differences when Amanda joined the Stanley family.

Some of the specific clues came from little things Molly or David's dad had let slip, but the strongest one came from one particular facial expression. The expression had been on Amanda's face the only time David had ever met her.

David had only met Amanda once because, in all the time Dad and Molly had been going together, Amanda had managed not to be around very much. Of course Dad had seen her; but whenever something was planned for both families, Amanda usually had something terribly important come up—like a test to study for, or a sudden attack of stomach flu. All but one time when they'd all gone to the zoo together, way back when Dad and Molly had first met.

David hadn't paid much attention to Amanda that afternoon because he had had no idea then that she was going to be his step sister, and besides he'd been busy keeping Blair away from the animals. Blair and most animals understood each other, so there really hadn't been too much danger—except from the zoo-keepers, who didn't understand about Blair at all.

David did recall saying "Hello" to Amanda when his father introduced them—and Amanda not saying anything. He could conjure up a vague picture of brownish hair and a red dress, but what he could remember best was the expression on Amanda's face. She had looked at him that same way every time he got near her all afternoon. It was the kind of look, that when people keep doing it at you, you start feeling you ought to check the bottom of your shoes—particularly when you're at the zoo. David had checked and his shoes were all right, but he hadn't forgotten that expression.

All of David's clues, and instincts, seemed to indicate that he should be prepared for almost anything, and he thought he was; he hoped he was. When Molly's little VW finally turned off the highway onto the long dusty driveway, David got up on his knees on the window seat and unlatched the window. He opened it just wide enough to see out through the crack. The glass in the old lattice windows was wavy and not much good for looking through when you were interested in details.

The car pulled up in front of the veranda steps, and for several minutes no one got out. David supposed that Molly and Amanda were in the midst of a discussion. Obviously they would have a lot to talk about. Since they'd seen each other, Dad and Molly had gotten married, gone away on a honeymoon, and come back and moved all their stuff and all the Stanley kids into the old Westerly house in the country—which happened to be the only house they could find that was big and cheap enough. And all that time Amanda had been staying with her own father in Southern California.

David was still waiting and watching when, in the room behind him, there was a loud clatter followed by a scream that sounded like a stepped-on cat. David could guess what had happened without even turning around. The last time he'd checked the kids, Janie had been building something in the corner, Esther had been cleaning the floor with her toy vacuum, and Blair had been curled up on David's bed fast asleep. Now Esther came running and climbed up beside David, and across the room Janie was standing up slowly with a clenched jaw and mean-looking eyes. Esther crawled behind David and peeked out at Janie who, as usual, was getting ready to throw things.

6

"Stop that, Janie," David said. "Put that down. What's the matter?"

"Tesser kicked over my horse corral," Janie said, between tight teeth. Tesser was what Esther had named herself before she could pronounce Esther.

"No," Esther said from behind David. "I didn't kick over it. I *fell* over it."

Janie kept coming. "Janie," David said, "if you throw that horse, you'll break it."

"You'll break Tesser," Esther said.

David laughed, and, after a moment, Janie looked at the china horse in her hand, and the red started going out of her face. David turned back to the window, thinking that Amanda was probably in the house and he'd missed seeing her, but she wasn't. Both Molly and Amanda were still sitting in the convertible. Just about then the door on Molly's side banged open, and Molly jumped out. She slammed the door behind her and walked fast across the driveway and up the steps, leaving Amanda sitting alone in the car. David couldn't see Molly's face very well, but something about the way she held her head and shoulders made him wonder if she were crying.

For another minute or two Amanda went on sitting in the car; but then her door opened very slowly and deliberately, and she got out. As soon as David got a good look at her, he leaned forward quickly, squeezing Esther into the corner of the window seat.

"Wow!" he said under his breath. Esther heard him and she shoved under his arm so that her face was under his in the crack of the window.

7

"Wow!" Esther said. "What's that?"

David didn't answer until Esther banged her head back against his chin and got his attention. "What's that?" she asked again.

"That?" David shook his head slowly. "That's our new sister, Tesser." And they both went on staring.

For the first second or two he'd actually thought there were a bunch of springs and wires coming out of Amanda's head, but then he realized it was only her hair. It seemed to be braided in dozens of long tight braids and some of them were looped around and fastened back to her head. The rest of her was almost covered by a huge bright colored shawl with a shaggy fringe, except for down below her knees, where something black with a crooked hem was hanging. She stood still for a minute after she got out of the car, looking after her mother; and David could see most of her face. He remembered, seeing her again, some things he'd forgotten— the very dark eyebrows, smallish nose, and the way her mouth moved now and then into what looked like an upside-down smile. But he didn't remember the spot in the middle of her forehead. It seemed to be shaped like a triangle, and when she moved, it caught and reflected the light like a tiny mirror.

She stood for a minute staring after her mother with her mouth in the upside-down smile, and then she turned back to the car. First she got out something that looked like a large dome-shaped cage covered with a beach towel, and then a couple of big suitcases. Next she opened the trunk and began lifting out boxes, lots of cardboard boxes that seemed to be filled with something very heavy. She put all the boxes and suitcases and the big cage together at the side of the driveway. She was getting two smaller cages out, when her eyes flicked upwards, and for a moment David wondered if she'd seen him in the crack of the window. But she only went on with what she was doing until everything was gathered together beside the driveway. She turned then, slowly and deliberately, and looked directly at David and Esther. There was no doubt about it. She went on looking long enough for David to be sure she really knew they were there, and then she nodded and made a motion with her hand. Both the nod and the wave meant, "Come here."

David jumped. He jumped back from the window and shut it. Esther looked up at him questioningly.

"That new sister said—like this," Esther said, making a "come here" motion with her hand.

"Yeah," David said. "I know." He opened the window again and leaned out. "Wha—who—d-did you want me?" he called.

Amanda tucked her lips in the upside-down smile and nodded, very slowly and definitely. She motioned towards the pile of boxes and bags. David got the point.

"Okay," he called. "I'll be right down."

"Right down," Esther said. She slid off the window seat, too.

David looked at her and frowned, but then he shrugged. If he stopped to argue with her, Janie would be sure to get interested, and Blair might even wake up and want to come along. And to have just one tag-along would be better than to have all three.

David nodded at Esther and said to Janie, "I'm going down to help carry boxes and things."

Janie only glanced at them and then went on rebuilding her

horse corral. David had put it that way on purpose, so as not to arouse her interest, and it worked. Everyone in the whole family was sick of carrying boxes and things.

On the way down the curving staircase David held Esther's hand because if you didn't she still had to put both feet on each stair, and it took forever; but as soon as they reached the bottom he pulled his hand away. He knew from experience that some people his own age thought it was funny the way the little Stanley kids followed him around and hung on him. Of course there was a reason for it—even before she died over a year before, their mother had been sick for a long time, and a lot of the time the kids hadn't had anyone else to hang on. But you couldn't go around explaining that to everyone.

David cringed inwardly remembering the time Esther had called him Mommy, right in front of a guy he used to know named Skip Hunter. Esther hadn't meant to, of course. She was very young at the time, and Mommy was one of the few words she knew. But Skip had made a big thing out of it, and a bunch of his friends had called David "Mommy" for a long time.

Esther was still tagging along, a few feet behind, when David went down the porch steps. He could see from there that the spot on Amanda's forehead was a triangle of some kind of metallic substance, which seemed to change colors when you looked at it from different angles. Amanda stood perfectly still watching them come, with only her eyes moving from David to Esther and back again—a long blank look from unblinking eyes.

"Hi," David said; but Amanda went on staring silently for so long that he began to wonder if she was still going to refuse to speak to him, even now that they had to live in the same house. It was so weird that David had to concentrate to keep his hands and face from doing nervous twitchy things while he waited.

At last Amanda sighed and said, "You're David," making the words a part of the sigh.

Because he was so glad to have the creepy silence over with, David nodded much too enthusiastically.

"And that one?" Amanda said, pointing at Esther. "Which one is that one?"

Because of the tone of Amanda's voice, David checked Esther out to see if there was something wrong with her, like maybe her nose was running or she'd forgotten some of her clothes; but everything seemed to be in order. Esther wasn't particularly gorgeous, but she looked about average for a four-year-old girl—short and solid with straight brown hair and fat pink cheeks.

"That's—" he started, but Esther drowned him out.

"That's Tesser," she said, pointing at herself right between the eyes.

"What did she say?" Amanda asked.

"She said Tesser," David said. "That's what she calls herself."

Amanda looked a little bit more interested than David had seen her look before. "Why does she do that?" she asked.

"I don't know," David said. "Why do you call yourself Tesser?"

"Because I am Tesser," Esther said.

"It's the way she pronounces Esther," David explained.

"Oh," Amanda shrugged, "is that all. I thought maybe it was her spiritual name."

"Her what?" David asked.

"Her spiritual name."

"Oh," David said.

Esther was jerking on the back of his shirt. He told her to stop and pushed her hand away, but she started in again. Finally he said, "What is it?" and she motioned with her finger for him to lean over.

"Whisper," she said.

David sighed. Esther never screamed and threw things like Janie, but she was terribly determined. He knew he might as well let her whisper or she'd go on asking for hundreds of times. He squatted down so she could reach his ear, and she leaned over and went, "Whizawhizawhiza," in it. You never could understand a word of Esther's whispers, but this time it was pretty plain what she meant, because she kept pointing at Amanda's head.

"I think she wants to know about your hair, or that thing on your forehead," he said.

"My hair?" Amanda said, as if there weren't anything unusual about it at all.

"Why it's all—uh, all in those tight braids."

"Oh that," Amanda said. "That's part of my ceremonial costume. So's this," she added, pointing to the triangle on her forehead. "This is my center of power."

"Power?" David was starting to ask, when suddenly Esther gave

12

an excited squeal. She had lifted the corner of the beach towel and was peeking into the dome-shaped cage.

"It's a bird," she said. "David, look. It's a great big bird."

"Yeah," David said. "It sure is. It looks like a crow. Isn't it a crow?"

Amanda picked up the cage and wrapped the towel back around it. "Not exactly," she said. "I'll carry the cages, and you can carry that box of books." She pointed to Esther. "And you carry that little train case."

The box of books was big and very heavy. David staggered a little going up the stairs. Behind him, Amanda was carrying the big cage in one hand and one of the little cages in the other. Behind them both, Esther came slowly, one step at a time.

When they got to the room that Molly had chosen for Amanda, David sat down on the box he'd been carrying to catch his breath. It was a small room but interesting, with dormer windows and a ceiling that slanted in all directions. Amanda looked around, blank-faced and cool-eyed as ever. David couldn't begin to guess if she liked the room or not.

He remembered then what he'd been about to ask before they started upstairs. "What did you mean—'not exactly'?" he said. "It's either a crow or it isn't. How come it's 'not exactly' a crow?"

Amanda unwrapped the beach towel, and the crow sidled across its perch and pecked viciously at her fingers. "It's not exactly a crow," she said, "because it's actually a familiar spirit. I don't suppose you've heard the term before, but this crow is my Familiar."

Chapter Two

DAVID DIDN'T HAVE THE SLIGHTEST IDEA WHAT AMANDA WAS TALKING ABOUT when she called the big black crow her Familiar. So, for a minute he just nodded, hoping she would go on talking long enough to explain. But instead she just stared at him with her lips going down and the end of one eyebrow going up.

"Haven't you ever heard of a Familiar?" she said, finally.

"Well," David said, "I think I've—it does sound kind of—" He stopped and grinned, "—familiar."

Amanda's lips flickered and flipped back down. She sighed. "That's an entirely different meaning," she said. "A Familiar is something that looks like an animal or bird, but really what it is, is a spirit. It's a spirit that lives with an occult person and is her contact with the world of the supernatural."

"The world of the supernatural?" David said. "What kind of supernatural?"

14

"Different kinds," Amanda said. "I've just begun to study, see, and I haven't decided yet what I'll specialize in. I have this friend, Leah, who's been studying for years, and she knows practically everything about the occult; but she's mainly interested in straight witchcraft. I haven't decided for sure. I'm considering different things."

"Like what, for instance?"

But just then Amanda noticed what Esther was doing. She had arrived, finally, while they were talking, and leaving the train case in the middle of the room, had gone directly to the crow's cage, near the window.

"Hey, get away from there," Amanda said.

David noticed then that all ten of Esther's fingers, plus the end of her nose, were inside the bars of the cage. She was saying something to the crow, but David couldn't hear what.

"Get away from there," Amanda yelled again. She jumped across the room and jerked Esther away from the cage. Esther stared at her with round eyes. "He'll peck you," Amanda went on shouting. "He'll bite the hell—" She caught herself and then went on. "You want your eyes pecked out?" She turned to David and shrugged. "Kids!" she said. "I'm just not used to them."

Esther ran to the other side of David and looked around him at Amanda. "Is that new sister going to throw things, too?" she asked.

"No," David said. "She's not mad at you. She just didn't want the crow to bite you."

"He didn't bite at me," Esther said.

Amanda made a snorting noise. "Listen kid, when that crow bites, he doesn't just bite at you. Look." She stuck out her hands. "See there, and there, and there."

There were several red scabby places on Amanda's hands and fingers. David looked at the crow. He certainly didn't look very friendly. He sat hunched over on his perch with his head pulled back into his shoulders and watched Amanda constantly with angry yellow eyes. Every time Amanda made a move toward him, his head would twitch forward and his beak start to open.

"How come he pecks you if he's your familiar spirit?" David asked, and immediately wished he hadn't. Amanda seemed to have a whole collection of cool expressions, and the one she gave David right then was one of the longest and coldest. "Because—" she said, and left a long silence that somehow managed to sound more insulting than words. "Because, I've only had him a few days. Leah says that I just haven't had time to establish communication. It takes time to establish communication, and it also takes the right kind of ceremonial rites. I've just started on them."

David crouched near the cage, and the crow slid closer, opening his beak in a very threatening way.

"Where did you get him?" David asked.

"In Santa Monica, just a few days ago. Just the day before I had to leave to come up here. It was very strange the way it happened." Amanda leaned forward and her eyes widened and flashed. "See—" she went on, glancing around in a secret furtive way and then dropping her voice to a tense excited whisper, "the weirdest part was that I'd just been reading this book about Familiars, only a day or two before, and then I just happened to go into this pet shop right near where my father lives, and as I walked in I heard a loud squawk, and I looked up and there he was looking at me—watching me wherever I went. As soon as I saw him, I had a strange feeling—almost like a vision—and I knew I had to have him. So that evening I told my dad about it, and he handed me the money to buy him—just like that."

David was fascinated. Watching Amanda's face as she talked about the crow was like watching one of those stone faces carved on mountains come alive, amazingly dramatically alive. David had been so busy trying to catch all of Amanda's expressions— mystery, suspense, excitement and several secretly significant looks that he couldn't quite interpret—that he'd almost lost track of what she was saying. He didn't catch on to the fact that he was supposed to respond until Amanda repeated, "He just *handed* me the money—just like that."

"He—he did?" David said. "How much did it cost?"

"About forty dollars."

"Wow."

Amanda shrugged. "My dad has lots of money. And he understood exactly how I felt about the crow. He always understands about my interests, like the occult and everything. And right after we bought the crow, we went to the travel bureau and exchanged the ticket Mom had sent me for one a day earlier so I could spend some time with my friend, Leah. We decided not to call Mom and tell her. I just took a taxi from the airport right to Leah's house, and then this morning I called and told Mom to pick me up there instead of at the airport."

"Yeah," David said. "I heard Molly talking to Dad about it at breakfast this morning, right after you called."

Amanda leaned forward. "Did you? What did she say? Was she mad?"

"I don't know if she was mad. She seemed kind of worried."

Amanda narrowed her eyes, but she didn't say anything.

They were on their way back downstairs to get another load of boxes and suitcases when it occurred to David to wonder where Molly was. He'd seen her run into the house, but he hadn't seen her since. It was strange she hadn't come up to help Amanda move into her new room.

"Where is Molly?" he asked.

"I don't know," Amanda said, and David noticed that she'd switched back to her usual stoney face. "Off somewhere being mad, I guess. We had a little argument, you might say, on the way here."

David just barely stopped himself from asking, "What about?" because it occurred to him that Amanda might say it wasn't any of his business. But he needn't have worried, Amanda seemed eager to talk about it.

"See, in the first place," she said, "my mother hates Leah, who is my very best friend. At least, she doesn't like me being friends with her. Leah has been my best friend for two years, ever since my parents got divorced and my mom and I moved into the same

18

apartment building with Leah and her mother. But my mother has always been against our friendship."

"Why?" David asked.

"Who knows?" Amanda said. They had reached the driveway, and Amanda was sorting out the things that were left there. The ones she was going to carry from the ones David was going to carry. David was getting all the boxes of books. "She never comes right out and admits that she hates Leah. She just mentions that Leah is older than I am, and that she is too wrapped up in the supernatural, and other things like that. And she doesn't like it much that Leah never talks to her."

"She never talks to your mother?" David asked. "How come?"

"Oh, it's nothing personal. I tried to tell Mom that. It's just that Leah doesn't have much use for adults. She doesn't talk to her own mother, either."

David almost forgot to listen for a minute because he was busy thinking about that—about someone who never talked to her own mother. But Amanda was going right on.

"Anyway, my mom was mad because my dad let me come early and stay overnight with Leah. She said she was worried about me arriving at the airport alone and getting a taxi by myself—but that's stupid. I always ride in taxis alone when I'm staying at my dad's. I've done it hundreds of times. Anyway, I had to go to Leah's because I'd left a lot of my stuff there."

David said, "I heard Molly say yesterday that she was going to stop at the apartment on the way back from the airport, to pick up your stuff."

"Sure, for a few minutes. But that would have been all. I wouldn't have gotten to see Leah at all. So my dad and I just changed the plans a little."

David nodded.

"But that wasn't what we were mainly arguing about," Amanda went on. "Mostly we were fighting about my clothes. She didn't want me to wear my occult outfit today."

"She doesn't want you to dress like that?"

"Oh, usually she doesn't say much about it. But she really had a fit today. Because I was coming here, for the first time and everything. She said I'd scare you kids to death."

"It didn't scare us to death," David said.

Amanda snorted. "Of course not. And it didn't matter a bit to her how important it was to me to wear my ceremonial robes today. See, today is a very important day for certain kinds of magic. Leah found out about it last night when she did a special ritual about the right days for contacting Familiars. We found out that I had to wear my robes and observe all the taboos and everything today, or I might never make contact with Rolor."

David opened his mouth to ask, but Amanda answered before he could. "Rolor is the name of my Familiar. It's a word of Power from an old magic chant about crows."

"Rolor is the crow's name?" David asked.

"Yeah. But I haven't started calling him that yet. I'm waiting until we establish communication."

"I'll bet you called him some other things when he bit you," David said.

Esther had finally reached the driveway, so Amanda started loading everyone up again. David had a second box of books, and Amanda had a suitcase and another cage. There wasn't anything small left so she gave Esther two of the books out of David's box. It was just as well because this box was even heavier than the first one.

When they got to the top of the stairs, David saw Blair and Janie coming down the hall from his room. They were just strolling along until Janie caught sight of Amanda. Then her face lit up like a switched-on computer, and she whizzed into Amanda's room dragging Blair behind her. By the time David tottered in after them, Janie was going full blast.

"Hello," she was saying. "I know who you are. I'm Janie Victoria Stanley, and I'm six years old, but I'm very mature for my age. You're Amanda Randall and you're twelve, and Molly is your mother so you're our sister now and—"

"Shut up, Janie," David said, and for a minute she did.

Amanda turned to David with a look he was beginning to recognize, although it still puzzled him. How did she manage to look so bored and disgusted without so much as twitching a muscle in her deadpan mask?

"What is it?" she asked. "A talking doll?"

David grinned. Janie was very small for her age and doll-faced cute looking. She had dimples and roundish blue eyes and long curly eyelashes, along with some other characteristics that Amanda would be finding out about before very long—like being a lot smarter and louder and more obnoxious than most six-year-olds.

David was sure that Amanda was going to find out some of these things almost immediately, and he was right.

"What's that thing in the cage?" Janie burst out again after being quiet for about one minute. "What's in the two little cages? What's wrong with your hair? What's that thing sticking to your forehead?"

Janie always asked questions faster than anybody could possibly answer them. Amanda didn't even try.

She did say, "It's a crow—and stay away from it," and "A snake and a horny toad—and stay away from them, too." But then she quit answering altogether and started putting clothing away in the dresser. Janie gave up after a while, sat down by Esther near the crow's cage, and started telling Esther all about crows. She told Esther what crows ate and the sounds they made and what scarecrows were for. That was another of Janie's habits. If she wasn't asking questions nobody could answer, she was answering questions nobody had asked.

Amanda just went on putting things away. Finally Blair came into the room from where he'd been standing near the door. He leaned against the dresser and smiled at Amanda. Amanda glanced at him and then looked away, but after a second she looked back. It was hard for most people to keep from looking at Blair, particularly when he smiled.

Blair was blond and blue-eyed like Janie, but with a different kind of face. Molly said that Blair had the kind of face you very seldom see on a real person. She said that she was going to stop trying to paint Blair's picture because no matter what style she tried to paint him in, he always ended up looking like an angel on a Christmas card.

After Amanda had looked at Blair several times she said, "Who are you?"

Blair's lips moved, but nothing loud enough to hear came out.

"Doesn't that one talk?" Amanda asked David.

"Blair talks," David said. "Just not very much."

"Well, that's a relief," Amanda said.

"He and Esther are only four years old," David said. "They're twins."

"Yeah," Amanda said. "I heard there were twins."

When they started back down for the last load of Amanda's things, they made all three of the kids come too, so they wouldn't be alone with the crow. Only one small suitcase and one box of books were left to carry in. The last box of books was the biggest.

"You sure have a lot of books," David said.

"I know," Amanda said. "Most of the ones in that box are a part of my supernatural library. You know—about black magic, spiritualism, astrology, witchcraft and stuff like that."

"Wow!" David said. Taking out some books for the twins and Janie to carry, he started having the good, slightly excited feeling that a library always gave him. Magic had always been one of his special interests, and he'd read lots of books on the subject, but he'd never seen most of the books in Amanda's box. The first two he picked up were called *Haunted Houses* and *Modern Witchcraft*. The cover of the witchcraft one had a picture of a blackish-red night sky with a pale moon crossed by thin snakey clouds.

"Wow," David said. "Could I borrow some of these?"

"Well," Amanda said, "I've never lent any of those books except to Leah. Besides, you don't seem like the type really."

"What type?"

"The supernatural type. What sign are you, anyway?"

"What do you mean—sign?"

"Huuh!" Amanda went. It sounded like a combination between a snort and a sigh. "Sign! Of the Zodiac. Your astrological sign!"

David shook his head.

Amanda snorted again, unbelievingly. "When is your birthday?" she asked with the kind of exaggerated patience that some adults use when they're explaining something to a kid. When David told her it was the second of October, she nodded knowingly. "That explains it," she said.

She picked up the last suitcase and started up the stairs. David came next with the box, and behind him the little kids each carried a couple of books. But even with the top layer of books out, the box was very heavy. David got as far as the landing before he collapsed.

"Go on," he said. "I'll be along in a minute." He slid the box onto the landing and then sprawled on his back beside it.

But Amanda sat down on the step above the landing and, of course, the kids stopped, too. Blair and Esther sat near David, but Janie stepped over his head, just missing his ear, and arranged herself on the stair above, next to Amanda.

"Don't you just love our new house?" Janie said. "It has a name. It's name is The Old Westerly Place. Did you ever live in a house with a name before? We never did. And it has sixteen and a half rooms."

David groaned. "It does not," he said. "It doesn't have that many rooms."

"It does too. I counted them myself. Yesterday I counted them. Didn't I, Tesser?"

"Well, you must have counted all the porches and bathrooms and everything then," David said. "Bathrooms and porches don't count."

"Bathrooms do too count," Janie said. "I counted them. And there are sixteen and a half. Don't you just love our new house? Don't you, Amanda?"

In the silence that followed David pushed himself to a sitting position. Amanda was staring at Janie with her chin on her fist. "New?" she said at last. "New house? It looks practically ancient to me."

"I know," Janie said. "It's extremely ancient, and David says it has secret passages and hidden treasures and ghosts, even."

Amanda looked at David.

David shook his head at Janie, thinking "you blabbermouth" but not saying it. "I didn't either" was all he said. "I only said that it was the kind of house that *might* have things like that."

"And David's been looking for them," Janie interrupted, "with a yardstick."

David stood up and started to pick up the box but Amanda sat still, not getting out of the way. "With a *yardstick*?" she asked.

David sat down again. "Well, I read about how you measure

walls in old houses. You measure on the outside and the inside, and if it doesn't add up the same there's probably a secret room or passage."

Amanda nodded thoughtfully. Still sitting with her chin on her fist she began to look around at the parts of the house you could see from the landing. There was a lot to see.

Right out in front of the landing and at almost the same level was the hall chandelier, and beyond that the fan-shaped colored glass window above the front door. When the sun was low, it shone through the glass and was spattered by the crystals of the chandelier into hundreds of shivering spots of red and green and gold. The front door was wide and thick and set in a carved frame of shiny dark wood. To the right and left, doors led into the living room and parlor and dining room, and if you leaned against the banisters, you could also see the kitchen door, farther down the hall.

The staircase itself was one of the best parts of the house. It was not very wide, but it was made of the same dark shiny wood, and the bannisters were elaborately carved. The fanciest posts were at both ends of each flight. They were carved to resemble a thick vine, twirling up to a huge wooden ball, and on each side fat wooden cupids reached up to touch the ball with chubby fingers. David's father said the banister was very unusual and in good condition considering its age. There were only a few places where the wood was chipped or cracking, and there was one cupid, there on the landing, who had a missing head.

David reached over and ran his fingers over the spot where the cupid's head should have been.

"Who did that?" Amanda asked.

"I don't know," David said. "We didn't. It must have happened a long time ago. See, somebody sanded off the place where it broke and varnished over it."

"We didn't do it," Janie said. "Somebody else did. Why didn't they just glue it back on, David. Why doesn't it have a head? Did it ever have a head?"

David sighed. "Sure it had a head. All the other cupids do. Watch out!"

Janie was stomping around over everybody's legs and fingers to get over to the cupid with the missing head. She squatted down with her nose almost touching it.

"Poor little cupid," she said in a soap-opera voice. David had a pretty good idea what was coming. Janie was going through a phase about gruesome things, the worse the better. "Poor little cupid," she said. "There it was, just playing with its little brother cupids, and along came this hungry giant with a great big ax and chopped—"

"Shut up, Janie," David said loud enough to drown her out because Blair and Tesser were both getting big eyed.

"And the poor little cupid's head fell off and it—" Janie went right on.

"Janie! Shut up!" David yelled. "That's not what happened, Tesser."

"What happened?" Esther asked.

"Well, the other cupids just took his head and hid it—for a joke."

"No," Janie said. "It was a horrible gi—"

"Listen, Janie," David said. He grabbed her shoulders and pulled her over backwards and sat on her and held her mouth shut. Sometimes it was the only way to get Janie's attention. "Listen, Janie. They took his head and hid it because he *talked* too much. That's what happens when you *talk* too much."

When Janie stopped sputtering and closed her mouth, David realized that he'd almost forgotten about Amanda, sitting there watching. He stole a glance at her as he let Janie up, but it didn't tell him anything. Amanda was still sitting there with her chin on her fist, watching all of them. There was something very mysterious about the way you could never tell what she was thinking.

Chapter Three

As soon as Amanda's things were all in her room, she went inside and locked everyone out. The twins wandered off downstairs and, after waiting around for a while outside Amanda's door, Janie started moving her horse corral to her own room. David went into his room and got out a book he'd been reading. He left his door open and pulled his big comfortable reading chair over to where he could see across the hall to the door of Amanda's room. He read for quite a long time, but she didn't come out.

Usually David enjoyed reading, and he was partway through a very good book, but that afternoon he had a hard time keeping his mind on the story. For some reason, he felt restless. Once, walking along the hall to the bathroom, he heard something in Amanda's room. It was low and rhythmical, and it went on and on in a kind of singsong.

A little later David decided he ought to go check on Janie, just to be sure she wasn't doing something she shouldn't. Of course, now that there was a mother in the family again, David didn't have to be responsible for the little kids anymore, at least not when Molly was at home. But he didn't mind helping out a little now and then. After all, he was certainly used to it.

So he walked past Amanda's door again, and the chanting sound was still going on. He stopped and was listening for a second, when the low singing sound suddenly broke off, and a voice said, "Ow!" very loud and clear. This was followed by a string of words that weren't quite as clear. But clear enough to get the general feeling.

It sounded like, "You mutter, mutter crow! I'm going to mutter, your mutter, mutter!"

Then there was a loud twang, as if something were hitting wire and a squawk and then footsteps. David hurried on down the hall.

When it got close to dinnertime and Amanda still hadn't opened her door, David gave up trying to read and went down to the kitchen. Molly was there peeling vegetables. She seemed to be feeling all right, although she was quieter than usual and her eyes looked a little red.

David said, "Hi" and stood around waiting. Usually that would be enough to get Molly started. Ordinarily, Molly was very talkative.

But she only said, "Oh, hi, David." And then after a long pause she asked, "Did you meet Amanda?"

"Sure," David said. "I helped carry her things up to her room."

"That was nice of you," Molly said. David waited, but she

didn't say any more about Amanda. Finally he went over and looked in the sink.

"Are you all through peeling?" he asked.

"No, there are the potatoes to do yet."

"Oh, I'll do that," David said.

Molly smiled a funny quivery smile, and for an uncomfortable second David thought she might be thinking of hugging him. So he explained quickly that he didn't mind peeling potatoes because he could peel them around and around to see how long a strip of peeling he could make without breaking it. So Molly went on with the rest of the dinner, and David finished the potatoes. While he peeled, he watched Molly, now and then, out of the corner of his eye.

Molly didn't seem much like a mother to David, but he realized this was probably because she was very different from his own mother. His own mother had been a very unusual person. There was a dreamlike quality to his memory of her, and it wasn't just because she had been dead for more than a year. She had always been a little like a person from a dream—beautiful and gentle and uncertain, and full of strange ideas about things that never happen to ordinary people.

Molly was entirely different. She usually wore bluejeans and baggy old shirts smudged with paint because she was an artist. She was very small and bouncy, and she wore her brown hair in a ponytail and went around with bare feet half the time. Everything except painting she did hard and fast, and a lot of the time it came out all wrong. When that happened she usually made a big joke of it, but once in a while she got really mad, for a minute or two.

David still wasn't really used to having Molly for a mother, but it didn't bother him now, not anymore. It had for a while. The way he felt about Molly had done a lot of changing. At first he'd thought she was great, when she and Dad were just friends and she'd gone places with the whole family and come over to cook dinner on the housekeeper's night off. He'd thought she was a lot of fun, the way she laughed and played with the little kids and treated David almost like a grown-up. But then, when he found out that she and Dad were thinking of getting married, he'd changed his mind for a while. He'd begun to notice other things about her. The way she yelled when she got mad and the way she dressed, and how she began acting as if Tesser and Blair and Janie belonged to her, instead of to their mother who hadn't been dead very long, even if they had almost forgotten her already. David hadn't forgotten her.

Finding the right house had been a big problem. They had to have something with at least four bedrooms and not very expensive. Molly had been looking for a long time before they found the Westerly place, and she could hardly believe it when they heard how big and cheap it was. It was later that they began to find out some of the reasons why it was so cheap.

One of the reasons was that it was so far from the city. But Dad said he didn't mind the commute, since college professors have odd schedules and he didn't have to drive at rush hour.

Another reason the house was so inexpensive was its age and condition.

It wasn't exactly that the Westerly place was run down. In the real estate office they told Molly that the old house was in amazingly good shape, and that was true in a way. Two old ladies had lived in the house all their lives and had always taken good care of it. They had kept it clean and painted and repaired. The main problem was that it hadn't been changed or remodeled a bit in probably more than fifty years. The bathrooms, for instance, still had pull chain toilets, and bathtubs that sat up high on iron eagle claws clutching round iron balls. Esther had really been impressed with those claws when she first saw them. She had looked and looked, and had even gotten down on her hands and knees to inspect them more carefully.

"What are those?" she had asked David.

"Those are its feet," David told her. "The bathtub's feet."

Esther backed away quickly and asked, "Do bathtubs walk?"

Of course Esther had just never seen that kind of bathtub before, and there were some things in the Westerly place that not even David had seen before. Like an icebox instead of a refrigerator, and a very noisy water heater that sat next to the woodstove and only heated when the stove was being used. In fact, Molly said that the whole kitchen in the Westerly house ought to be in a museum someplace and that was exactly where it was going as soon as she could afford something to take its place. Molly said that she'd always loved old houses, but trying to learn to cook for a big family in that kitchen, after having only Amanda to cook for in a modern apartment, was enough to send a person into shock.

Molly was setting the big round table in the middle of the kitchen—for seven people now that Amanda was there—when they heard Dad's car in the driveway. Molly ran out to meet him. David heard her say, "Oh Jeff, I'm so glad you're home. What a day—" and then her voice got lower, and he couldn't hear anymore. They stayed outside for several minutes longer. When they came in, David's father was saying something about Amanda; but before David could get the drift of the conversation, the twins came in from outdoors and Molly changed the subject.

Amanda was late coming down to dinner. Janie began talking about her the minute she sat down at the table.

"Amanda's here," she told Dad. "We helped her carry her things up to her room."

"So I heard," Dad said.

"She has a crow that's very dangerous, and a snake and a horny toad, and she has special clothing for doing magic cere-monies in and—"

Janie stopped suddenly, and everyone looked up and saw Amanda standing in the door of the kitchen. She was still wearing her ceremonial robes and absolutely no expression, except for a trace of her upside-down smile.

"Oh, hi," David said, and then everyone else at the table started saying hello, too. After it had been quiet for a second, Blair said a soft short "Hi," like the last little clink at the end of a long clatter.

Amanda didn't say anything. She only looked around at all of

34

them; it was a long, cool, critical look. David had seen almost exactly the same expression on Molly's face when she was looking at a really bad painting. But on Amanda, the expression seemed to be almost built in. She even managed to chew and swallow without changing it enough to notice.

The only thing Amanda said during the meal was "yes" and "no" when Dad or Molly asked her a direct question. And for a while no one else said much either. Usually the only conversational problem around the Stanleys' table was everyone trying to talk at once, but that night there were long, nervous, quiet spaces.

Finally Molly asked Janie what she'd been doing all afternoon, and Janie started telling about her horse corral and the personalities of all the china and plastic and imaginary horses that lived in it; and for once it was almost a relief to listen to Janie. It was probably the first time in her life that Janie had ever gotten through a meal without being told to be quiet at least once.

That night in bed, David stayed awake for quite a long time thinking, mostly about Amanda. He thought about the slow, cool way her eyes turned towards Dad when he spoke to her. It reminded David of the way Skip Hunter had always looked at Mr. Endicott, the sixth-grade teacher, even when Mr. Endicott was yelling at him.

Skip had lived two houses away from the Stanleys' old house in the city, and he had really been more of a neighbor than a friend; but he and David had spent some time together on weekends. Skip used to come over to look at David's reptile collection. But then David had to get rid of the collection because the second

housekeeper after his mother died had been really hysterical about snakes. After that Skip quit coming because he really had liked the snakes better than David. Actually David hadn't liked Skip very much either, but he was interested in Skip in a way, because everyone else was.

Everyone was interested in Skip because he had the biggest reputation of anybody in the school. He had been suspended four times and arrested twice; and in the fifth grade, he had given the teacher a nervous breakdown. Everyone said that Skip was the coolest kid in the school—and it was probably the truth.

Once, David had decided to make a project of watching Skip to find out about being cool. He had decided that being cool was never being embarrassed or nervous or bashful. It was also never taking anything, or anybody, very seriously. It was particularly cool to be bored when other people were taking themselves seriously, whether they were being seriously enthusiastic, or excited, or angry. After studying Skip all semester, David felt sure he understood about being cool. The only thing was—he couldn't do it. As a matter of fact, Skip told a lot of people that David was as uncool as you could get—and that was probably true, too.

Blair was awake for a while that night, too. After they'd both been lying there for a long time, Blair sat up and looked over at David.

"David," Blair said, "that crow."

Blair had a way of saying what he was going to talk about before he began, as if he were giving it a title.

"Yes," David said. "What about the crow?"

37

"That crow is angry."

"Yeah, I guess it is," David said. "What do you think it's angry about?"

"I don't know," Blair said. "But it's very angry."

After Blair finally went to sleep, David got out of bed and stood in front of the mirror. He stood sideways and then turned very very slowly and deliberately, giving the mirror a long slow look. He did it several times, but it never was just right. It would take a long time and a lot of practice to develop a thing like that. He wondered how long it had taken Amanda.

Chapter Four

Breakfast the next morning was a lot like dinner the night before, at least as far as conversation was concerned. Amanda was looking quite different because she was wearing jeans and a shirt instead of the occult outfit and all the braids were combed out into frizzy waves; but she was just as silent as ever. When Dad or Molly spoke to her, she waited before she answered. First, she waited before she looked at them, and then she waited staring right at them, and then, one split second before you were sure she wasn't going to answer at all—she said something. Something—but never very much.

David was a little puzzled by the way his father was behaving. Jeffrey A. Stanley, Assistant Professor of geology at Amesworth College, had had a lot of experience with kids of all ages. He was a large man with a strong thin face, and there was a very firm look about him that seemed to impress most people. Not that he was mean or unreasonable. David usually thought his father was pretty fair and understanding. He did have a temper though, and definite opinions, and he wasn't the kind of person you could stare in the eye with a what-are-you-going-to-do-about-it expression on your face. Not ordinarily.

Dad seemed to realize that David was puzzled, because he managed to explain things a little before he left for school. After he kissed Molly and Janie and Esther goodbye, he asked David to help carry some things out to the car. He did have a few books and a briefcase to take, but nothing he couldn't have managed himself, so he obviously really just wanted a chance to talk to David alone.

On the way to the garage, which, at the Westerly house, sat back from the house and still had a hayloft because it had once been the stable, Dad asked, "Well, what do you think of your new sister?"

"Well," David said. "She's pretty interesting. I mean, I don't think she's going to be boring or anything. But she certainly has a mind of her own, doesn't she?"

His father smiled. "True," he said. "She very definitely has a mind of her own. But we have to remember that she's a bit upset and unhappy right now and—"

"You mean about you and Molly getting married?" David said.

"Yes, that's part of it."

"Yeah," David said. "Well, I didn't like it much either when I first heard about it, remember? Until I got used to the idea and got to know Molly better and everything."

"That's right. But it's different for Amanda, and a little harder, I think. Her own father is still alive and that makes it more complicated for her. She's been through some difficult times in the last few years, and now she has this new adjustment to make. It's not going to be easy for her, and it may not always be easy for the rest of us. It's going to take some extra effort—and a lot of patience."

David grinned. "Yeah," he said. "I know what you mean. Like the way she was at breakfast. If one of us kids acted that way, you'd really blast us."

Dad laughed. "You're probably right. And if she keeps it up, I may blast Amanda a little, eventually. But for the time being I'm trying to remember to be patient. And I hope you kids will, too."

David looked his father right in the eye, "Sure," he said. "Sure, Dad." He really meant it, too, but at the same time he wondered what it would be like to look at Dad that way and not say anything, or even smile.

David went on standing there, wondering, while his dad backed the car out of the garage—and that was a mistake. Part way down the drive the car stopped, and Dad rolled down the window.

"I almost forgot," Dad said. "Would you get started weeding the flower beds in front of the house? The ones we were watering on Saturday. Remember?"

"Yeah," David said. "I remember."

"Get started on them this morning, all of you. Tell the twins and Janie to help, too. Tell them I said you were all to work for a while before anyone starts playing."

"How about Amanda?"

41

"We'll leave that up to Molly. But I should think Amanda could help, too."

Dad backed on down the driveway, and David sighed. It wasn't the weeding itself he minded so much as the part about getting Janie and the twins to help. He'd been that route before. Getting that bunch to work together on something was like having one of those dreams where you keep running and running and never getting anywhere. Besides, David had been hoping to talk to Amanda before she locked herself in her room again. He wanted to talk some more about the supernatural and maybe get a chance to look at some of her books. He really doubted if she would be helping with the weeding.

Back in the kitchen, when David made the announcement about the weeding, Janie and the twins couldn't wait to get started. They'd never weeded before, and they were always enthusiastic about anything new—at least, for the first couple of minutes. Amanda was still sitting at the table saying nothing.

"You run along and help for a while, too," Molly said to her, and Amanda just went on saying nothing.

David looked at Molly, and Molly looked at Amanda, and Amanda looked at her plate. Then Molly took a deep breath and went over to the table and took Amanda by the arm. "Get up from there this minute and go outside and help!" Molly said in a very angry voice.

Amanda stood up slowly, jerked her arm away, and walked out the door after Janie and the twins, and David followed. He didn't look back at Molly.

David had to make a detour to the garage for the tools so the rest of them were already milling around the garden when he got there. All except Amanda, who was curled up on the wrought iron garden bench. David walked around inspecting things, trying to decide who should do what. The ground was soft and damp because Dad had been soaking it since they moved in. The real estate agent had said the old Westerly ladies had kept beautiful gardens, but everything had been neglected during the time the house was up for sale. Now, flowers and bushes that had been almost dead were coming back to life, but there were weeds everywhere.

"Tesser and Blair," David said, "you're too little for the hoes, so you'll have to pull the weeds up by hand. You do this little place over here, just up to the rose bushes. And Janie you take this next—"

But as usual, Janie had her own ideas. "I want to do those big thistles out by the fence," she said.

"But that's the hardest," David said. "You're too little."

"I'm not! I'm not too little. I want to do the thistles!"

David sighed. It was his own fault. He should have had better sense than to tell Janie she was too little for something. He picked up a hoe and started in on the place he'd planned to give to Janie, and Janie marched out to the thistle patch. At least, David told himself, he'd had enough sense not to try to tell Amanda what to do. That would really have been embarrassing. It was bad enough just having her lounging there on the bench watching everything through narrowed eyes, smiling the upside-down smile.

Inwardly David shrugged his shoulders. Let her do what she

wanted, it wasn't any of his business. He'd done what Dad told him and that was all he was going to do. He'd gotten the kids started, but from now on they were on their own. If they didn't do it right, and they probably wouldn't, he wasn't going to say a thing. Not with Amanda lying there watching him.

David turned his back on everybody, put his mind on his hoeing, and worked hard. It must have been about five minutes later that he heard a weird sound and straightened up. It sounded like a wailing scream, and it seemed to come from the thistle patch. He looked that way in time to see Janie staggering out of the thistles waving her hoe in one hand and clutching her chest with the other. She staggered a few more steps and collapsed on the ground. David was starting to run towards her when she jumped up again.

"What's the matter, Janie?" David called.

"I'm fighting a battle," Janie called. "See, the thistles are the enemy soldiers and I'm the good guys and the hoe is my sword. And I rush in and attack and slay them. Only when a thistle touches me then I'm slayed."

"Slain," David said, walking over to take a look. A few of the thistles were chopped off at various heights and a few more were just bent over. David started to mention that at the rate she was going it was going to take a hundred years of war to get rid of the thistle patch, but then he remembered. He'd done what he said he would and that was enough. If Dad wanted to turn Janie into a gardener, he'd have to do it himself. David went back to his area, and Janie waved her hoe and charged back into the thistle patch, yelling at the top of her lungs.

44

David went on working. The twins did, too. They pulled up one weed at a time and then stood up and walked very slowly to the edge of the garden and put it down, and went slowly back. While they were walking, they were watching the battle in the thistle patch. David clenched his teeth to keep from saying anything and went on hoeing.

When he had cleared a large area and his back and hands were beginning to hurt, he straightened up. Nobody else had accomplished enough to notice, and Amanda was still sitting on the iron bench. David went over and sat down on the bench, too, being careful not to look at Amanda. He wasn't going to be the first to say something, in case she wasn't speaking to him today either.

He sat for a few minutes resting his back. In that time Blair carried the same weed back and forth several times before he remembered to put it down, and Tesser quit working altogether and just stood there watching Janie. David didn't really blame the twins too much. As usual, Janie was being extremely noticeable. In about five minutes David watched several noisy galloping charges through the thistle patch, and a couple of violent deaths complete with horrible gurgling noises and final twitches.

"They're not getting a whole lot done, are they?" Amanda said suddenly, and David almost jumped he was so surprised to hear her voice.

"You can say that again," he said, shaking his head. "Nobody can make that Janie do anything. Not unless it's her own idea anyway. I mean, nobody."

There was a long pause before Amanda said, "I'll bet I could."

"How?" David asked.

"Oh, I don't know. I'd have to think about it. But I bet I could."

David shrugged skeptically and went on watching what was probably supposed to be a wounded horse. Janie was galloping around making whinnying noises and leaning over farther and farther to one side.

When the horse finished dying Amanda said, "You want to see me?"

David had gotten so intrigued by Janie's dying horse technique he had forgotten what they were talking about. "See you what?" he asked.

"See me make Janie do something."

"Sure," David said. "Help yourself."

Amanda looked back towards the house very carefully. There was no sign of anyone watching. Then she yelled, "Hey kids!"

Esther and Blair came right over, but it took two or three louder yells to reach Janie over the noise of battle.

When she had everyone's attention, Amanda said, "Okay kids, we're going to play a new game. It's called Slaves and Slavedriver."

Amanda was the slavedriver. She took off her belt and tied it onto a stick for a whip. Then she made everyone pull weeds, and she marched up and down whipping and yelling, "Faster! Faster!"

It worked for quite a while. Everyone pulled like mad, and Janie had a great time moaning and suffering when she got whipped. Amanda's belt was only made of cloth, so it didn't really hurt; but it was easy to pretend it did because Amanda swung it so hard and so much like she meant it. It made the game exciting enough to keep everyone interested for a long time. By the time Janie began to demand a chance to be the slavedriver, an amazing amount of garden had been weeded.

When the front door opened suddenly and Molly came out on the porch, Amanda handed Janie the whip and strolled back to the bench. David went over to talk to Molly. Molly was amazed at how much work had been done.

"Yeah," David said. "Dad'll be surprised."

"He'll be very pleased. Did Amanda help?"

"Sure," David said. "She helped a lot."

Molly went over to the bench and said something to Amanda and patted her on the shoulder. From the porch, David couldn't tell for sure, but it didn't look as if Amanda said anything.

Afterwards Janie went on playing slavedriver with Blair and Tesser as slaves, and David took Amanda on a tour of the property. He showed her the little grove of very old trees behind the house and the dry creek bed at the very end of the lot. In the stable-garage he showed her the old mangers where the horses used to eat, and the loft up above. They sat for a while in the loft and talked.

"Why did you tell my mother I helped?" Amanda asked.

"Because you did," David said. "We'd never have gotten half as much done if you hadn't thought of that slavedriver business."

Amanda made her snorting noise. "Big deal," she said. "I wasn't trying to get the weeding done. I was just practicing my powers. An important part of being an occult person is developing your power over other people. I just wanted to see if I could make them do it."

"Well you sure did," David said.

Amanda shrugged. "There's nothing to it once you've developed your powers."

"What was wrong with telling your mother you helped?" David asked. "She would have been awfully mad if you hadn't."

"I don't care," Amanda said.

David stared at her. "Why not?" he asked.

"Because I hate her. That's why not."

"You hate Molly?" David could hardly believe it. Molly just didn't seem like the kind of person anyone would hate. You might feel as if you could do without her maybe, but there wasn't anything much about her to hate.

"I hate her," Amanda said, "because she divorced my father."

"My dad said they divorced each other," David said. "They kind of agreed on it."

"Well, that's not what my dad says, and he ought to know. She divorced him, and then when I was almost getting used to living with Mom in our apartment and had a friend and everything, then she goes and marries your father, who's practically poor and has a whole bunch of kids for her to take care of that aren't even hers, and we have to move out here to the country where I can't see Leah anymore, and I'll have to go to some crummy old country school where there won't be anybody who's anything like me, and everybody will hate me."

48

"Wow!" David said, and then after a minute he added, "My dad isn't poor."

"Well, he is compared to my dad."

"How do you know?" David asked.

"Because my dad told me so."

"Oh," David said. "Did he tell you all that other stuff, too?"

"He didn't have to tell me that. I knew it already. But we talked about it. My dad understands how I feel. He doesn't blame me for being mad."

David only nodded because he couldn't think of anything else to say, and after a while Amanda said, "I'll bet your dad doesn't like the supernatural, either. I'll bet he hates it. Doesn't he?"

"No," David said. "I don't think he hates it. He usually just smiles when we talk about anything like that."

"See!" Amanda said fiercely. "That's just what I meant."

"My mother really liked it though," David said. "In fact—" David paused and looked at Amanda, "—she was a little bit that way herself. Supernatural, I mean."

"Yeah?" Amanda said. "Like what?"

David said slowly. "Well, she believed in ghosts and spirits, and she talked to animals, and she liked anything that was strange and fantastic. I think she knew about things that hadn't happened yet, too. At least sometimes."

"Your *mother* believed in things like that?"

David nodded.

"Weird," Amanda said.

But David was busy thinking about what he had said—about

49

the ways in which his mother had been supernatural. He was remembering that she believed in good omens, like rainbows and church bells. And that she was always finding magical messages in ordinary things. He remembered too, about her premonitions— how she sometimes seemed to know about things that were going to happen. After she died, David had realized that she had probably known she was going to die a long time before anyone else did. David knew because, looking back, he could see that she had started getting him ready to help his father take care of the family, way back before anyone else knew that she was even very sick.

Suddenly, what Amanda had said registered with David.

"Weird?" he asked. "What's weird about being supernatural? I thought you were yourself."

"Well sure," Amanda said. "It just seems like a weird thing for your mother to be."

Chapter Five

Dᴀᴠɪᴅ ᴡᴀs ʙᴇɢɪɴɴɪɴɢ ᴛᴏ ғɪɴᴅ ᴏᴜᴛ ᴛʜᴀᴛ ᴛʜᴇ ᴏɴᴇ ᴛʜɪɴɢ ʏᴏᴜ ᴄᴏᴜʟᴅ count on with Amanda was surprises. After they'd had the long conversation in the loft of the garage, and talked about their mothers and other important subjects, David thought he'd gotten to know her, at least a little. But the next time he spoke to her, she made a face as if she were about to throw up and slowly and deliberately turned her back on him. David didn't get it! He didn't get it at all—except that Molly happened to be coming into the room just then and that probably had something to do with it. Later, the evening of that same day, David was sitting on the front steps, looking out across the lawn that was beginning to turn green again, when Amanda came out of the house and stood right in front of him.

David looked at her warily until she smiled and said, "I'm going herb hunting. Want to come along?"

She started off so fast that David almost had to run to catch up. "Herbs?" he said. "What kind of herbs?"

"Oh, the usual thing."

"You mean for cooking?"

"No, stupid. For magic. Some herbs have magical powers. You need herbs for nearly every kind of spell or potion or philter. Leah buys hers at an herb store, but out in the country you can pick your own if you know what to look for."

"What kinds are you looking for?"

"Oh, wolfsbane and deathcup and bloodroot—things like that."

"Where are you going to look?"

"Well, a cemetery would be the best place. You don't know of one around here, do you?"

"No," David said. "Not around here."

"I didn't think you would. I was planning to look along the sides of the road. That's a pretty good spot. Particularly if you know of a place where someone died. Or at a crossroad. A crossroad is a good place for all sorts of supernatural things."

The nearest crossroad was almost a half a mile away, and when they got there Amanda looked around and picked some sprigs off several plants. It seemed to David that the stuff she called wolfsbane was just plain old anise, and bloodroot looked a lot like ordinary Queen Anne's lace. Amanda got excited, though, when she found it.

"Are you sure that's wolfsbane," David asked, "because it sure looks like—"

"Look!" Amanda said. "I've used wolfsbane hundreds of times and it always looks and smells just like this, except drier, of course. Leah gets it at the herb store, and it costs about $5.00 for just a few leaves. Leah says it's very rare and expensive."

David guessed Leah must have known what she was talking about, but he wished he'd known you could sell that weed—whatever it was—for that much money.

On the way home, carrying her bag of herbs, Amanda talked some more about Leah and the things she did. Leah had studied palmistry, and at school she had set up a noontime palm reading service. Because palmistry is a very complicated thing to learn and Amanda had only begun to study, she usually collected the money, fifty cents a palm, and kept track of the scheduling of clients, while Leah did the readings. Amanda was also in charge of talking to the kids who were waiting their turn, to discover who might be interested in buying a love philter or a curse.

"How much did those cost?"

"That depended," Amanda said.

"On what?"

"On how much allowance the kid got. And on how much they wanted to get even with someone or make someone like them. Some of the love philters we got a whole dollar for. The curses were usually a little cheaper."

"You must have made a lot of money."

"I didn't. Leah kept most of it."

"How come?" David asked. "Why didn't you get half?"

"Because most of the supplies we used were Leah's, and

54

besides she was always broke because her father never paid his child support. But I was going to get to keep some of the money after I'd finished all my rites of initiation. Then, just when I got everything learned, I had to leave."

"And Leah never did give you any of the money?"

"No," Amanda said. "It was just that she needed a lot of money to buy all our supplies, and it was hard for her to get any with a deadbeat father and a mother she wasn't speaking to. And we didn't make any money on some of the magic we did. Like the time we broke Mr. Fitzmaurice's leg. We didn't do that for money, at all."

"What did you break his leg for?"

"Revenge," Amanda said.

"Revenge?"

Amanda nodded. She pulled her dark eyebrows together in an expression that made David think of the way the crow looked at Amanda. "To get even with Mr. Fitzmaurice for being an unfair and prejudiced person. See, Leah had a paper to write about the Aztec Indians for history class, and Leah got this very good student named Millicent Endicott to let her copy hers. Millicent had a different teacher for history, so no one could have known about the copying. Then"—Amanda paused and made her face say you-won't-believe-this-and-it-will-make-you-furious—"then, Millicent got an A on the Aztec Indians and Mr. Fitzmaurice only gave Leah a C-. On the very same paper! Leah was furious. I mean, after all the time it took to convince Millicent about the evil eye and what it could do to you, and then on top of that all the work of copying the paper, which was

55

very long, and then to only get a C-! It really proved that Mr. Fitzmaurice was a very prejudiced person."

"Why was he prejudiced against Leah?"

"Who knows?" Amanda said. "Except that the only people he wasn't prejudiced against were a few types who did all their homework and laughed at his corny jokes. Anyway, we got a hair off the shoulder of his jacket, and we put it on a clay doll, and then we stuck pins in the doll, and very soon afterwards Mr. Fitzmaurice went skiing and broke his leg."

David couldn't help being impressed. Amanda could look you right in the eye and start telling you something that sounded impossible, and by the time she got through telling it, it didn't seem impossible at all.

"Wow!" David said when Amanda got through telling him about Mr. Fitzmaurice.

Amanda looked pleased. "Hey," she said, "how'd you like to take some lessons in the supernatural? The little kids could, too, even. You could all be my neophytes."

"What's a neophyte?" David asked.

"A learner. Somebody who's new at something. I was Leah's neophyte until I passed the initiation, so now all you kids could be mine."

David was really surprised when Amanda invited him and the kids to become her neophytes. He'd been hoping she'd tell him some more about the supernatural, and maybe let him read some of her books, but he certainly hadn't expected to be a part of any of her supernatural ceremonies.

Actually David hadn't made any very positive decisions concerning Amanda and her magic. He hadn't decided just how supernatural he thought it really was, for instance, and he really hadn't tried to decide. He wasn't sure why, but he remembered once he'd asked his mother if she believed in ghosts, and she'd said that she didn't disbelieve in anything that made the world more exciting. David decided now that he felt the same way. And there was one thing you had to say for Amanda—she usually made the world more exciting, one way or another.

That night, as they were going to bed, David told the kids about Amanda's invitation, and they were all enthusiastic. Janie talked about learning to be a witch, and David told her he thought she had a pretty good start already. Esther kept chattering about rabbits. At first David couldn't figure out what she was talking about, until he realized that he'd said Amanda was going to teach them how to do magic. Apparently Esther had gotten the idea from somewhere—TV probably—that magic consisted mostly of pulling rabbits out of tall black hats. And Esther had always been crazy about rabbits.

Blair didn't say very much, as usual, but David could tell he was interested. Finally he said, "David?" and when David looked at him he said, "David, what *is* magic?"

David hadn't realized before how hard it was to explain magic with nothing but words. "Well," he said, "it's when you do things other people can't do, by using powers that other people don't have."

Blair nodded, smiling his Christmas card smile. "Oh," he said. "Is *that* magic?"

"But you have to study for a long time and do all sorts of ceremonies and spells to get the powers."

Blair looked puzzled. "You *have* to do spells?" he asked.

David nodded.

"Does Amanda do spells?"

"Sure. Lots of them."

"David," Blair said, "when Amanda has a spell, does she kick the crow?"

"Kick the crow?" David said, but then he laughed, because he remembered that one of the housekeepers had called Janie's tantrums "having a spell."

"Not that kind of a spell, Blair," he said. "And Amanda doesn't kick the crow."

Blair shook his head. "She does," he said.

Esther interrupted them with another question about rabbits, and David went back to explaining that there might not be any, at least not right away.

Early the next day Molly went to the village to do some shopping, and as soon as she was gone Amanda called all the Stanleys into her room. The room looked very different from the way it had looked when David had seen it last. There were bright colored posters all over the walls, and in several places strange looking objects hung from the ceiling. One of the things looked like a huge eye painted on cardboard, and some others seemed to be made of sticks and yarn. There were long strings of beads hanging in front of the window, and curtains hanging in several places inside the room. There was a curtain over the door to the closet and another

manda threw the card down. "See," she said to David, "what
tell you. He just doesn't get it."

avid went over and picked up the card. It was the nine of
. Just at that moment Amanda gave a little scream, and for a
econd David thought she was just surprised because Blair
what the card was. Obviously Blair had not only known that
rd was red—he had known it was hearts and that there were a
them. He would probably have known it was nine if he had
how to count that far. David was just opening his mouth to
that Blair had always been a little strange about things like
hen he noticed what Amanda was really screaming about. The
was out of the cage.

e crow was hopping across the floor on its big black feet, and
ngs were spreading out wider and wider. As they all stood
, watching, it jumped into the air, and Amanda screamed
It flapped madly around the room, with its huge wings mak-
awful racket. It lit once for a second on the dresser and
ed over a bunch of bottles and jars, then took off again. When
lly lit on the middle of the bed, Janie and David and Esther
manda were all lying on the floor. Amanda had her arms
er head. They all sat up slowly and cautiously.

air walked over to the bed. When the crow saw him, it bobbed
d up and down and came towards him in two big floppy
Blair put his round babyish arms around the crow and lifted
e bed. It was so big for him that he had to walk leaning back-
The crow hung limp, with its head bobbling and its huge

one draped down the front of the bookcase. In the center of the
room was a card table with a shawl over it and a deck of cards in
the center. Amanda was wearing her black dress and shawl, and
she had the shiny triangle glued on her forehead, but her hair
wasn't braided. As soon as they were all inside, Amanda shut the
door and sat down at the table. There was one other chair, on the
other side of the table. David and Esther and Janie sat down on
the edge of the bed, and Blair went over and sat on the floor near
the crow's cage.

Amanda picked up the cards and began shuffling them. "I've
decided," she said, "that before I can start teaching you, I have to
give you some tests."

"Like I.Q. tests?" Janie said. "I have a very high I.Q."

"No, not like I.Q. I'm going to test you for supernatural apti-
tude. I'm going to find out if any of you have any natural psychic
talents. Some people are just naturally born with telepathy and
things like that, and there are tests that are done in laboratories to
find out who's got it. Leah and I read all about it. I don't really
think any of you guys have any, or not much, at least. But this way
we can find out for sure. You're first, David. Sit down in the chair."

The test was to find out how good you were at reading other
people's minds. Amanda held the cards one at a time so that
David couldn't see them, and David was supposed to say whether
she was looking at a red card or a black one. Amanda explained
that an ordinary person could be expected to guess correctly about
half the time, or about ten right out of twenty cards. If you got as
many as fourteen or fifteen right you were pretty psychic. When

Leah had given Amanda the test, Amanda had had fourteen right, the first time.

So Amanda held up the cards with their backs to David and David guessed red or black. When he was finished, Amanda said he'd gotten eleven right, which wasn't very good, but not quite hopeless. Janie was next.

Janie insisted on taking a long long time to guess each card. Each time she put her forefingers against her forehead on each side and rocked back and forth with her eyes shut, murmuring, "red or black, red or black." Then when she got one wrong, she went into a long argument about how she had meant to say the other color only it had come out wrong when she said it, so she ought to get another chance. Once while David was waiting for Janie and Amanda to stop arguing over whether a mistake ought to count, he happened to notice what Blair was doing.

Blair was feeding something to the crow. It looked like liverwurst and it probably was, because Blair loved liverwurst and he was always carrying pieces of it around in his pockets. David thought of warning Blair to be careful, but the crow didn't seem to be interested in biting anything but the liverwurst, so he didn't bother. Besides, Blair was usually able to take care of himself where animals were concerned.

When Janie was finally finished, her score was thirteen, only she kept saying it was really fifteen, except Amanda didn't count it right. Esther was next. She climbed up into the chair and got all settled with her fat legs sticking out in front of her and her hands folded in her lap. She closed her eyes as Janie had, and then she

opened them again and said, "If I win do I get to rabbit?"

"Rabbit?" Amanda said. "What's she talking abou

David tried to explain, and Amanda snorted a with the test. When she had finished, Esther's score wa

"Did I do good?" Esther asked Amanda.

"You did just ordinary. Nothing special," Amanda

Esther came over and leaned against David.

"David?" she said, looking very sad.

"Look, Tesser," David whispered. "If there are ever an you'll get one. I promise."

Esther grinned and climbed back up beside him on of the bed. David noticed that Amanda was putting th away.

"What about Blair?" he asked.

Amanda looked surprised. "How can he do it?" she sai doesn't even talk."

"He talks!" David said. "I told you he talks. Just not ver

"Well, I've never heard him," Amanda said.

Blair went over to the table and looked at Amanda.

"Well, all right," she said. "Get in the chair." She pu card and stared at it.

Blair climbed up into the chair and sat very still, Amanda and smiling.

"Well, what is it?" she said at last. "Is it red or bla

"It's valentines," Blair said in a very soft voice. "I tle valentines."

curled-up claws hanging almost to the floor. Blair walked slowly to the cage and put the crow inside.

Amanda jumped to her feet. "Wow!" she said. "It's tame. All of a sudden it's tame. You know what it must be? It must be because it got a chance to get out and fly a little. It probably was mad because it never got to fly anymore. That must have been what made it so mean." She went over to the cage and opened the door and stepped back. The crow came out.

It came out with a rush and took off. It flapped and beat its way around the room several times, making a feathery roar and brief but violent little windstorms. Everyone began ducking and squealing. Finally it lit again on the bed. Amanda walked towards it.

"Rolor," Amanda said. "Rolor—obufo—luaul—ofubo—rolor." The crow edged away from her.

She walked around to the other side of the bed and moved slowly towards it, saying the strange words very softly. The crow started to sidestep back across the bed.

All of a sudden Amanda lunged and grabbed with both arms. There was a loud squawk and an explosion of arms and claws and feathers. The crow seemed to be clawing and flapping its way right up the front of Amanda, while Amanda ran towards the cage, grabbing and hitting at the crow. When she got to the cage, the crow was on top of her head with its claws all tangled up in her hair. She jerked it off and threw it into the cage so hard it hit the other side. Then she hauled off and kicked the cage as hard as she could. The metal wires went twa-ang-ang-angg and every one of the crow's feathers seemed to stand on end and vibrate. The crow squawked, and Amanda said, "It serves you right you—mutter—mutter—mutter!"

When Amanda turned around, her hair was standing on end, her face was red, and there was a long scratch down one cheek. She just stood looking at David and the kids for a minute, breathing hard. Then she brushed at her hair and gave a little shrug. "Crazy crow," she said coolly. "Something must have scared it." She walked over to the table, picked up the cards and started putting them away. "You can go now," she said. "That's all we're going to do today. We'll do some more tomorrow."

David and Blair and Esther started for the door, but as usual, Janie had to argue.

"Can't we stay?" she asked. "Can't we stay and learn some more. I want to stay and learn some more about taming the crow."

"Get out!" Amanda said.

Chapter Six

AMANDA DIDN'T LET THEM BACK INTO HER ROOM UNTIL THE NEXT DAY.
When she did, the card table had been put away and instead there
was a candle and a metal bowl full of burning incense in the middle of the floor. The windows were closed and the drapes pulled
and the sweetish smoke swirled in the dim light. Amanda had
them all sit down on the floor around the candle and incense.

"Today we're going to begin the initiation rites," she said.

"The what?" Janie asked.

"The rites of initiation," Amanda said slowly and distinctly.

All three of the little kids still looked blank. "Look," David
said, "it's like in that fairy tale I read you about the prince who
had to do all sorts of trials and tests before he got to marry the
princess. In an initiation you have to do trials to prove you're
good enough to do—whatever you're getting ready to do."

"Dibs on David," Esther said.

"What do you mean dibs on me?" David asked.

"To marry. I get to marry David."

Amanda and Janie laughed. "You dope," Janie said. "You can't marry your own brother. You aren't even old enough."

"Besides it's not that kind of an initiation," David explained. "We're being initiated into the supernatural." He looked at Amanda for confirmation.

Amanda nodded. "Into the world of the occult," she said.

"Into magic!" Janie said.

"Ooooh!" Esther said in a now-I-get-it tone of voice. "Dibs on the first rabbit."

Amanda ignored her and went on with the explanation. It seemed that there were going to be nine tests. Amanda called them ordeals. Each ordeal would last for a whole day. If you passed one ordeal, you got to go on to the next one; and if you didn't pass, you had to do it over again on the next day. When they had all passed all the ordeals, there would be a ceremony of initiation. The final rite of initiation would be very complicated and difficult, and when it was over they would be members of the occult world.

"There are some things you'll have to start doing right away in order to be ready for the rites," Amanda said. "I mean, besides the ordeals. For one thing, you all have to start right away collecting things for your ceremonial clothing. Because that's something you can't do at the last minute. It took me weeks and weeks to get all my things together. I'll tell you about it now, so you can get started. First of all, every thing has to be very old, the older the better. Like my black dress. I found it in a junk store, and the clerk said it was a real antique. Besides that, at least one of the things you wear has to have belonged to a dead person. And one of them has to be stolen."

"Stolen?" David said. "Who has to steal them?"

"You do. Each one has to steal his own."

"We have to steal?" Janie asked, looking amazed. David knew why. His father had a lot of very firm ideas about stealing, and Janie had heard all of them, many times.

Amanda nodded.

"You have to steal so you can be in the rite of initiation?" Janie asked.

"Yes!"

Janie thought about that for a while and then she asked, "Do you ever have to be in a wrong of initiation?"

"Look kid," Amanda said. "Do you want to hear about this or don't you? There's one more thing about your robes. You can't wear anything white."

"Not even your underpants?" Janie asked.

"Not any of it," Amanda said, glaring first at Janie and then at David. "If you don't shut her up, we're never going to get started."

"Shut up, Janie," David said.

After that Amanda explained the first ordeal. The first one was that for a whole day they couldn't wear or let anything made of metal touch their skin. It was going to start at midnight that night and last until the next midnight.

When David first thought about it, it seemed easy. But then he began to realize some of the problems.

"How do you turn on the faucets?" Janie asked.

"That won't be too hard," David said. "Just wrap a towel around your hand first. Wouldn't that be all right?"

Amanda nodded. "Yeah," she said. "But you haven't thought of the hardest part yet. How about mealtimes. You have to eat everything with your fingers."

"Molly won't like it," Esther said.

"I'll bet she'll let us, just for one day, if we explain about why we're doing it," David said. "Molly isn't very fussy about—"

Amanda was shaking her head back and forth and looking disgusted.

"What's the matter?" David asked.

"You don't know anything about how fussy she is. She's not your mother. Besides, you're not allowed to *explain* it. If you explain that you're doing an ordeal, it ruins it. It ruins the whole ordeal, and you have to do another one instead."

"Wow!" David said. "Why not? Why can't you at least tell your own family about it?"

Amanda arranged her face in an insulting sneer. "Look *Davie*," she said, "it's just that wizards and sorcerers don't usually go running to ask their mommies—"

"Okay, okay," David said. "I just wondered, that's all."

The rest of the day, in between working in the garden, taking the kids for a hike, and doing some reading, David did some thinking about the next day's ordeal. He came up with some good ideas and some others that turned out to be useless.

He thought, for a while, that he had solved the mealtime problem when he remembered the plastic spoons Molly kept for picnics, but when he went to look for them they had disappeared. When he asked Molly about them, she said she couldn't understand it because she was sure they'd been there a day or two before. Molly looked through the drawer herself after David gave up.

"That's strange," she said. "Perhaps the kids took them."

When David told her that he'd already checked with the kids and they hadn't, Molly shook her head. "Well," she said, smiling at David, "it must have been our ghost, then."

"What ghost?" David asked.

"Ours," Molly said. "An old house like this one surely must have at least one ghost, don't you think."

"Oh sure," David said laughing. It was the first time he'd ever heard Molly say anything about ghosts, and he was sure she only meant it as a joke. Afterwards he wasn't so sure.

It wasn't until quite late in the afternoon that the zipper problem occurred to him. It was his problem mainly because the girls had lots of clothes without zippers and Blair had some boxer type pants with only elastic. David checked over his wardrobe and decided that the safest thing for him to wear would be his swimming trunks, even though, unless the weather warmed up, they might be a little hard to explain.

By bedtime that night David had metal on the brain. He had taken the kids on a last minute tour of the house pointing out all the things that were made of metal, but he wasn't sure they'd remember everything. Like, for instance, the metal doorknob on the kitchen door when most of the doorknobs were okay because they were of crystal.

David was still lying in bed, waiting to go to sleep, when suddenly he had a bright idea. The first big problem was going to be breakfast. Dad liked to get up early so he had time for a leisurely breakfast with the whole family before he left for work; and if there was one thing he was strict about, it was having things polite and peaceful at the table. If everyone started eating with their fingers, things would get unpeaceful in a hurry. There was just one possibility that might simplify things.

Molly who, unlike Dad, tended to be careless about routine things, had forgotten a couple of times to set the alarm clock. And on those days she had hurriedly made Dad's breakfast and gotten him off to work before she called the rest of the family. Once she'd even asked David to be in charge of the kid's breakfast afterwards, so she could get started on her painting. David hadn't minded because he'd done it all the time before Dad and Molly were married. That kind of situation would make things a lot simpler in the morning. The tricky part would be getting Molly to oversleep.

David jumped out of bed suddenly and went out into the hall. Upstairs everything was very quiet but the lights were still on downstairs, so Dad and Molly were still up. David went down as far as the landing and listened. He could hear the sound of voices in the living room, so he went back up the stairs quickly and down the hall to Dad and Molly's room. On the night stand was

Molly's alarm clock. David set the alarm hand for about forty-five minutes later than usual. That would just about give Dad time to make it if he swallowed his breakfast in a hurry. It was a dirty trick to play on Molly, but David excused it by thinking it probably wouldn't upset her and Dad as much as watching everybody eating their corn flakes with their bare fingers. This way Molly would just rush around and get Dad off, and then David would offer to feed the kids so Molly could get to work at her painting. It ought to work like a charm if Molly just didn't notice that the alarm setting had been changed before she went to bed that night.

It worked fine. David woke the next morning to the sound of Molly's feet almost running down the stairs. When he checked the time on his watch, sure enough, she was good and late. A few minutes later he heard Dad's footsteps, slower, but hurrying, too. David got up and looked out the window to see if the weather was cooperating, too. It wasn't particularly. It was overcast, and a little bit windy.

In his swimming trunks David felt definitely chilly, so he put on his heaviest sweatshirt. He was hoping that would even things up, but what it did was make one end too warm and the other too cold. That didn't worry him, though. It was almost sure to get warmer later in the day, and besides, he reasoned, he probably shouldn't expect an ordeal to be too comfortable. Not a really good ordeal, anyway.

Next David got out Blair's clothing so he wouldn't forget and touch the metal drawer pulls on his chest of drawers. Then he went in the girls' room and got their clothes out, too. When he got down to the kitchen, Dad was just leaving. As soon as he drove off, Molly poured herself some coffee and collapsed into a chair.

"I really don't know what's the matter with me, David," she said. "I would almost swear I didn't touch that clock last night, and it was all right yesterday. But this morning the alarm was set for almost an hour later. Either the clock is going crazy, or I am."

"Do you suppose a person could fool around with a clock in his sleep?" David asked.

"Well, I suppose it's possible, but I've never done anything like that before. The other times I overslept I forgot to pull out the switch so the alarm just didn't go off. It went off this morning all right—only a lot too late."

David shook his head sympathetically. "Hey," he said, "how about my fixing the kids' breakfast this morning so you won't have to be so late starting on your painting."

Molly smiled and shook her head slowly in a kind of unbelieving way. "David, you are, without a doubt, the—"

She stopped suddenly, looking towards the kitchen door. "Good morning," she said.

It was Amanda. She came in and sat down at the table. "You know what I'd like?" she said to Molly. It was the first time David had heard her say something to an adult who hadn't just asked her a point-blank question. "I'd really like some pancakes for breakfast."

"I'm going to make breakfast," David said.

"Can you make pancakes?"

"I don't know," David said. "I never tried pancakes."

"Well, I sure would like some pancakes," Amanda said, almost smiling at her mother.

"I think I could take the time to whip up some pancakes," Molly said. "I'll take you up on your offer some other day, David."

Molly got busy on the pancakes, and David got a chance to whisper to Amanda. "Hey, you really blew it. I had it all fixed up so she wouldn't be around while the kids ate breakfast."

Amanda looked at him blankly. "Look," she said. "I happened to feel like pancakes. Get the picture?"

"Yeah," David said. "I get the picture." And he really did, at least a little. He was just beginning to get the picture about Amanda and the ordeals.

Chapter Seven

WHAT DAVID BEGAN TO REALIZE THAT MORNING, WHEN AMANDA INSISTED on pancakes, was that she wasn't going to be the least bit helpful in getting all the Stanley kids through the ordeals. As a matter of fact, David was beginning to think she might be planning to make it just as hard for them as she possibly could. David wasn't sure why she wanted things to be so difficult, but he was starting to have a theory or two about it. And it didn't all have to do with the supernatural.

Whatever the reason, Amanda had fouled up his breakfast arrangement, and something else had to be done in a hurry. David decided to go upstairs and try to slow the kids down. Instead of letting them go to breakfast as soon as they were dressed, he took them all into his room and gave them a long lecture on all the things he'd taught them the day before about metal. All the time he was talking Janie kept saying she knew it already, and Esther kept saying she was hungry, and Blair just daydreamed, looking out the window. David didn't mention the pancakes, because he knew that if he did he couldn't have kept them in the room a minute—ordeal or no ordeal.

Finally, when he was sure that Molly must have finished cooking the pancakes, David decided to let them go. Just as he got out of the door, he heard Molly calling.

"David," she called. "Where is everyone? The pancakes are getting cold."

"Pancakes!" the kids yelled and rushed around David and down the stairs so fast that David almost had to break his neck to get back in front of them. At the kitchen door he stopped, and Janie ran into him with a thud, followed by two little bumps when Blair and Esther ran into her.

"I finally got them ready," David said, strolling into the room. "Sorry we're late. Why don't you go on and paint now. I can do the rest."

As soon as Molly had gone, David picked up all the silverware in a dishtowel so the kids wouldn't forget and touch it. Then he buttered and jammed all the pancakes with a rubber plate scraper and let the kids eat them with their fingers. It worked fine with just jam, but Janie insisted on having syrup, too, and the whole thing got very messy. Cleaning it up afterwards, it seemed to David that everything in the whole kitchen had gotten sticky—except the silverware, of course.

The middle part of the day went pretty smoothly because lunch was only sandwiches and fruit. For a while the weather was even warm enough to make most of the goose bumps on David's bare legs disappear. But there was still dinner to worry about. When it was almost time for Dad to get home, David still hadn't come up with any general plan. Finally, in desperation, he decided that it would have to be every man for himself. He found the kids sitting on the front porch and told them so.

"Look," he said. "I can't think of any easy way to do it. I can't find the plastic spoons, and Molly says that if we wanted hamburgers we should have told her sooner because she has things all planned for tonight. So, you're all going to have to think up your own way to do it. I give up."

"What are you going to do?" Janie asked.

"Well, the best thing I can think of is just trying to eat with my fingers when they're not looking, but it probably won't work. In that case I'll say I have a stomach ache and get excused from the table."

"You'll starve," Esther said.

"No I won't. Not from missing one meal," David told Esther, but she didn't look convinced. Esther had never missed even a part of a meal in her whole life, so she certainly didn't know much about starving.

"Maybe I'll have a stomach ache, too," Janie said. Missing a meal wouldn't be any problem for Janie. She was one of the fussiest eaters in the world, and lots of meals she barely ate anything.

"Okay, Janie," David said, "I'll let you have the stomach ache. It's more your kind of thing. I'll think of something else." He hadn't been too enthusiastic about it anyway, since Molly was fixing lambchops, which happened to be one of his favorite foods.

Just then Amanda came out of the house, and David changed the subject. He had a feeling that it wouldn't be smart to let her know their plans ahead of time. She went on hanging around, so, when David got a new idea—and a good one—a few minutes later, he wasn't able to share it with the kids.

Dinner got off to a bad start. For one thing, David's father had just gotten home from work and—as anyone knows who has had much experience with parents—that's the very worst time to be annoying. Especially if several people are annoying in quick succession.

All three of the little kids were late getting to the table. They'd been sent to wash their hands and, of course, the problem of coping with the metal faucets had slowed things up. Everyone else was at the table, and Dad was looking impatient when finally Janie and Blair came in, and right after that Molly got up and closed the kitchen door because it was making a draft. She had no more than gotten back to the table when there was a knock on the door.

Dad frowned and called, "Esther. Is that you?"

"Yes, it's Tesser," Esther answered through the door.

"Well, come in."

There was a pause, and then Esther yelled, "I can't." David was thinking she could use her skirt to cover the metal doorknob, but then he remembered she was wearing slacks. He picked up his napkin and started to go to the rescue.

"Sit down, David," Dad said and he shoved his chair back and went to the door and jerked it open. Esther strolled in innocently while Dad turned the doorknob back and forth and checked the catch.

"There's nothing wrong with this doorknob, Esther," Dad said. "Did you turn it before you pulled on it?"

Esther looked at Dad blankly for a moment, and David held his breath. Then she just shook her head and said, "No."

"You didn't?" Dad said. "Well, next time try it, will you? Just turn the doorknob and *then* pull."

About one minute later, Molly sent David to get the butter and Dad noticed the swimming trunks. As a general rule, people didn't wear swimming suits to the dinner table in the Stanley household. Dad was starting to remind David of that fact when David interrupted to explain that he'd been planning to help the kids play in the sprinkler, only the day never did get quite warm enough.

"I should think not," Dad said, and then almost immediately afterwards he added, "Janie, what on earth?"

Janie was eating her dinner, using her regular spoon and fork, *only* she was wearing a huge pair of very fuzzy rabbit fur mittens. Janie had gotten the mittens for Christmas, but she'd never worn them much because they were so thick and clumsy. Janie's spoon looked as if it were sticking out of a huge ball of white fur, and her lips were pulled way back in a kind of snarl, so only her teeth would touch the metal spoon.

Janie smiled brightly at Dad, making her eyes and dimples twinkle like the little girl in the toothpaste commercial on TV. "My hands

78

are cold, Daddy," she said in a cutesy voice. "My hands have been very cold all day. I must be catching something." She wrinkled up her nose and sneezed a very phony sneeze.

Dad looked at David and back at Janie. Then Molly laughed, and Dad finally grinned too, shaking his head.

"You must have been having some rather peculiar weather around here today," he said.

"Very peculiar," Molly said, filling Blair's plate and passing it back to him. "Highly variable."

After that, for a short interval, things went smoothly. Dad began telling Molly about a field trip he was going to go on; and for a little while they were so busy talking, they didn't notice what was going on around the table. It was a good thing, too, because all sorts of strange things were happening.

David put his last minute plan to work, and in less than thirty seconds, with his eyes on Dad and Molly the whole time, he cleaned up his entire plate. Just before dinner he'd put a plastic vegetable bag in his pocket, and as soon as no one was looking, he simply got it out and dumped his whole dinner into it. Later he would sneak it out and eat it in the privacy of his own room. He didn't much like the idea of having everything all mixed together, but it would be better than no dinner at all. With his own dinner safely disposed of in his lap, David had a chance to check out the other kids.

Janie was doing fine with her fuzzy mittens. David wondered why he hadn't thought of mittens or gloves. But of course, it wouldn't have worked for all of them to do it. Janie might be able

to get away with mittens and curled-back lips, because she was always doing weird things. But it would have ruined it for everyone to try it.

Esther was eating her peas with something that looked like a little shovel. David leaned closer and recognized it as the coal shovel from her doll house. Fortunately everything in the doll house was made of plastic. The shovel made a pretty good spoon, except that it only held about two peas at a time.

Blair was simply eating everything with his fingers. David knew that Dad would put an end to that in a hurry, as soon as he noticed, but for quite a while he didn't. He and Molly were so wrapped up in their conversation that for several minutes they didn't notice anything at all.

"But Jeff," Molly was saying, "how will we manage for three whole weeks without you?"

Blair had nearly finished his mashed potatoes, Janie was struggling to cut up her lambchops with her rabbit paw hands, and David's mashed potatoes were making a very warm spot on his leg, when Amanda suddenly sat her glass down with a loud bang.

"Well, I don't have to accept," Dad had been saying, "but the extra money—" He stopped and looked at Amanda. Everyone looked at Amanda.

"I almost dropped my glass," she said.

Dad nodded but his eyes, in traveling back to Molly, unfortunately took in a few other things.

"David," he asked, "what happened to your dinner? Did I forget to serve you?"

"Uh no," David said. "You didn't forget. It's—it's all gone already. I guess I was pretty hungry."

"You must have been. Would you like some more?"

"Oh no," David said, squirming a little because the spot on his leg directly under the mashed potatoes and gravy was beginning to burn. "I've had plenty thanks."

"Did you eat the bones, too?" Amanda asked all of a sudden.

Janie glared at Amanda. "Yes he did," she said. "He ate the bones, too. David has very strong teeth."

David smiled uneasily. "I don't think my lambchop had any bones," he said. "I must have had a boneless one."

Dad was looking at David with a strange expression, but then he noticed something else. Blair was finishing up his peas by rolling a kind of snowball of mashed potatoes through them, and stuffing the whole thing into his mouth with very gooey fingers.

"Blair," Dad said, "what are you doing?"

Blair swallowed and licked his fingers and swallowed some more. Then he smiled his soft serious smile and said, "I'm eating with my fingers."

"That much I can see," Dad said. "What I'd like to know is *why?*"

Blair wrinkled his forehead and tilted his head thoughtfully. Blair always did that before he answered a question, but this time David could tell that Dad wasn't in the mood to be as patient as you usually had to be with Blair.

"Why I'm eating with my fingers?" Blair asked.

"Exactly," Dad said, and his voice was like the last sizzle of the fuse before the bomb exploded.

Blair's face wrinkled again and very very slowly he said, "I . . . have . . . to."

"What do you mean—you have to? Why do you have to?" Dad's voice crackled frighteningly, and for a minute everyone sat very still looking at him. Even Amanda glanced up at Dad, just an instantaneous flick of a look, but it made David think of something Janie did with her eyes just before she jumped three of your men in a checker game.

Then Molly put her hand on Dad's arm. "Jeff," she said, "about the field trip—"

Dad looked at her and back at Blair. "Well, stop it right now, Blair," he said. "Don't eat with your fingers anymore."

Blair nodded and stopped eating entirely. Fortunately he was almost finished, so that a little later when Dad had a phone call and Molly was getting the dessert, he was able to quickly clean up the last little bit with his tongue.

While Dad and Molly were away from the table, David whispered to Janie to help Esther out, because if Esther went on eating with the coal shovel it was obviously going to take all night. As usual, Janie overdid it. She picked up a spoon in her mittened hand and, with a terrible snarl on her face, to show Esther how to keep her lips from touching the metal, she shoveled half a plate of food into Esther's mouth in about half a minute. Looking scared to death, probably by Janie's snarl, Esther kept opening her mouth even when she wasn't ready for another bite. She had always been a good eater, but nobody could be that good. A minute later, when Molly asked her if she wanted a cupcake, she erupted like a volcano and started turning blue.

Molly screamed, "Jeff, Esther's choking!" and Dad came running in from the hall. By the time Dad and Molly had finished jerking Esther's arms up above her head and pounding on her back, everyone else had finished their cupcakes and were ready to leave the table.

At first it seemed to David that, as an ordeal, dinner had been a big success. It had been very difficult, and everyone had done it in his own way, and everyone had passed.

David was feeling very good about the whole thing until Janie asked Dad if everyone was excused to leave the table. Dad and Molly were just stitting there, staring into their coffee cups; and when Janie asked, Dad said, "Yes. Yes, by all means."

That was all he said, but there was something about the way he said it that made David start looking at things a little differently. What he started thinking was, that dinner had been a different kind of ordeal than he'd thought—a different kind, at least, for some people. But there was an expression on Amanda's face as she strolled out of the kitchen that made David wonder if she hadn't intended exactly the kind of ordeal it turned out to be.

That night during his usual time for thinking things over—when he was lying in bed waiting to go to sleep—David thought some more about intentions.

He decided that Amanda was really serious about believing in magic, no matter what else she intended when she asked the Stanley kids to join the world of the occult. He also decided that perhaps he had a few secret intentions himself in wanting to be a part of whatever it was Amanda was planning. Maybe he had a few intentions he hadn't told anyone about—not even himself—at least, not entirely.

There was one thing he was sure of, however, about his intentions. He really intended to pass all the ordeals Amanda could think of, and then—well, he'd just see what happened next.

Chapter Eight

THE NEXT MORNING DURING BREAKFAST, DAVID FOUND OUT MORE ABOUT the field trip that Dad was going to make. It seemed that Dr. Bradley, who was the head of Dad's department at the college, had been sick and his doctor had told him he couldn't lead a field trip into the mountains that summer. But the students were all signed up and all the arrangements had been made, so he wanted Dad to take his place as the leader. Dad had planned to take the second semester of summer school off, and now he was not only going to have to teach all summer, but he'd have to be away in the mountains for three whole weeks.

David could tell that neither Dad nor Molly were very happy about it, but they explained that they'd decided it was the only thing to do. Partly for Dr. Bradley's sake, but also because moving had been a lot more expensive than they'd anticipated, and because a few things around the house were going to need some rather expensive repairs before winter.

"I'll say," Janie said. "Like that upstairs toilet. You know what happens sometimes when you pull the chain?"

"Yes, Janie, we know," Dad said. "You told us all about it in great detail just the other day. And if you remember, at that time we discussed a few general rules for mealtime conversation."

But Janie went right on talking. "But Amanda didn't hear about it," she said. She leaned towards Amanda and, over the sound of Dad's voice you could hear Janie saying things like, "whoosh" and "all over the floor," until finally Dad roared, "Janie!" and everything got quiet.

Then Molly mentioned how great it would be if they could afford a new furnace before winter, and David reminded everyone that the hot bath water usually wasn't. So it was obvious that they could use the extra money Dad would get for leading the field trip.

"And I'm counting on all of you to be helpful and responsible while I'm gone," Dad said.

Everybody agreed that they would be except Amanda, who just sat there smiling her upside-down smile.

After breakfast Amanda told David and the kids to come outside because she had to talk to them. When they were all sitting on the back steps, she started walking up and down in front of them, talking while she walked.

"Today," she said, and David could tell immediately that she was in one of her dramatic moods. "Today we are going on a safari to hunt for reptiles."

After the announcement there came a significant pause, but Janie interrupted it by asking, "Why don't we just walk down to the creek? There are a lot of snakes down there."

Amanda went right on, "The second ordeal, which starts tomorrow morning, and which will be much harder than the first one, will require that every neophyte have a reptile. Every neophyte must have a reptile and carry it on his person from sunup until sundown."

"Carry it where? Carry it where, David?" Esther asked excitedly.

"On your person."

Esther looked down at herself before she asked, "If I don't have one could I put it in my pocket?"

"Shhh!" David said. He couldn't help smiling, but it wasn't just at Esther. He was smiling because if Amanda thought this ordeal was going to be a very hard one, she was in for a surprise. With a geologist for a father, the Stanley kids had all been on hiking expeditions and had gotten used to wildlife very early. In fact, at one time they'd had a whole collection of reptiles in their basement, until they had to get rid of it because the housekeeper they'd had then had had a serious allergy to crawly things.

"What kind of reptiles do we need?" Janie was asking. "Any old kind or something special?"

"Snakes would be best," Amanda said, "but other kinds will do. Lizards or horny toads or frogs."

"Frogs aren't reptiles," Janie said. "Frogs are amphibians."

"Or frogs!" Amanda repeated in a tense voice.

"I wish we still had our African Sun Gazer," David said. "It was a special kind of lizard we had once. It had spines all over it, like a miniature dragon."

"Could we catch one around here?" Amanda asked.

"No," David said. "They come from Africa. Dad bought ours at a pet store."

"Your dad bought it? Does he like reptiles?"

"Sure," David said, puzzled.

Amanda paced up and down for a while longer, and then she said, "I've been thinking, and it seems to me that it's a little too early for the reptile ordeal. It seems to me that it really ought to be about the fifth or sixth ordeal, instead of the second."

"Why?" David asked.

"Well, for one thing, we probably won't be able to catch enough in just one day."

"We can try," David suggested. "Then if we can't find enough we can always put it off until we do. It looks like a good day for a reptile hunt—nice and sunny."

Amanda finally agreed that they might as well have the hunt, and decide later about when to have the ordeal. David sent the kids off to collect jars and paper bags, and while they were gone he had a chance to talk to Amanda.

"How'd you like the way we all passed the ordeal yesterday?" he asked. "I'll bet you never thought we'd all make it on the first day."

Amanda shrugged. "Anybody can get through an ordeal, if they don't care how they do it."

"What do you mean 'if they don't care how they do it'?" David asked. "What was wrong with the way we did it?"

"Well, in the first place," Amanda began, "well, it's hard to explain exactly. There are just right ways and wrong ways to do things that are supernatural. I mean, it's supposed to be *mysterious* and *dignified*."

"Mysterious," David said. "Like what?"

"Like—mysterious. I guess you just have the feeling for being mysterious, or you don't. Like for instance, can you imagine a real wizard, like Merlin or someone, wearing *bunny mittens*?"

"Look," David said, "the ordeal was not to touch metal for a day, right? So we didn't touch it. So we passed, right?"

Amanda just looked at him. "You passed," she said, finally. "You just don't understand what I'm talking about."

"I understand," David said. "I just don't see why it matters."

"It matters," Amanda said.

The kids came back then, loaded down with hunting equipment, so the expedition got under way. They started out for the creek bed, where there were always lizards, and sometimes a snake or two.

"But since we're looking for them, we probably won't see any today," David said. "That's usually the way it is."

"Yeah," Amanda said, "I doubt if we can catch enough."

Suddenly something occurred to David. "Hey," he said, "you

already have one snake and the horny toad. If we don't catch enough today, couldn't two of us use them?"

Amanda shook her head. "No," she said. "They might get away from you and get lost."

"Well, we could catch you some others later on, to take their place."

"Nothing could take their place—ever!" Amanda said, and her voice reminded David of Janie's when she was being very tragic about something.

David could tell he was supposed to say, "Why not?" so he did.

"Because my father gave them to me," Amanda said.

"Where did he catch them?" David asked. "I thought he lived in the city?"

"He does. He bought them for me at the pet shop. He gave me the money and let me pick them out. I'd wanted a reptile pet for a long time, and my mother wouldn't let me have one, so once when I went to see my father I told him about it, and he gave me the money to buy them. My father always lets me have anything I want."

"Anything?" David asked.

Amanda nodded. "He's the only person in the world who really cares about me, and he's the only one I care about."

"Why don't you live with him, then, instead of Molly?" David asked.

"He'd like to have me, but he can't. Because he doesn't have a wife to take care of me."

91

"Why doesn't he get a housekeeper then. That's what my father did."

"He has a housekeeper. She's just not the kind who takes care of kids. And besides, my father's terribly busy because he works very hard, so I wouldn't get to see him much. Even when I go to visit, he doesn't have time to see me very much."

David shrugged. "Well, I don't see why you'd need somebody taking care of you. You're twelve years old already. I don't see why your dad couldn't let you live there, if he really wanted to."

Without any warning at all, Amanda whirled around and shoved David so hard that he went backwards over a big rock and landed sitting down.

"Hey!" David yelled.

The kids, who had been running ahead, stopped and came back to see what had happened.

"Shut up," Amanda sizzled between her teeth at David. "Shut up talking about my father. Don't you ever mention him again."

"Wow," David said, getting up and dusting off the seat of his pants. For a second he considered shoving Amanda back, but there was the fact that she was a girl, and besides there was all that stuff he'd promised his father about *patience*. So instead he just said, "Wow, I didn't mention him. You mentioned him."

David told the kids that he'd fallen down, and they went on down to the creek together and began the hunt. Amanda walked behind David not speaking again until she forgot about it in the excitement when they caught the first lizard.

The first lizard was a large bluebelly, and not long afterwards they caught a very tiny one, hardly more than two inches tail and all. Then, a long way down the creek they spotted a small gopher snake. There was a mad chase that lasted for several minutes before the snake caught himself by running into Blair's paper bag.

Amanda pulled away when David opened the top of the bag to show her. "Are you sure it's not a poisonous one?" she asked.

"No, it's a gopher snake," David said. "Dad taught us how to tell."

Amanda peeked in gingerly, jumping when the snake hissed.

"I thought you loved snakes?" Janie said.

"I do," Amanda said. "It just surprised me when he made that noise. It's really stupid to be afraid of snakes."

By the time the snake was captured, it was almost noon, and it was very hot and dry in the creek bed. Esther began saying it was time to go home for lunch. So they decided to look for the last reptile on the way home. They didn't see a single thing however until they stopped at the water faucet in the back yard for a drink. And there on the damp brick near the faucet was a salamander.

"I'll take him," Janie said. "I like salamanders."

David was willing. He wasn't crazy about salamanders himself, because of the sliminess. "But a salamander's really not a reptile," he said.

"He's all right," Janie said. "Amanda said a frog was all right, and a frog's not a reptile, either. Isn't he all right, Amanda?"

Amanda leaned forward to look at the slimy bulgy eyed creature squirming around in Janie's hand. Her lips turned down and her shoulders gave a quick little shudder. "Sure," she said. "He'll do fine."

The reptile ordeal began the next morning as soon as everyone got up. The little lizard and the salamander were small enough to fit easily inside a pocket, so wearing them all day was not much of a problem for Janie and Esther. Blair's large lizard and David's snake were a little harder to carry. Finally David dressed himself and Blair in long sleeved turtleneck shirts, with the shirttails tucked into tight belts. Then they put their reptiles inside their shirts and stood in front of the mirror to see what would happen. In about a minute the snake was poking his head out the neck hole right under David's left ear. David shoved him back down, but in another minute Blair's lizard was doing the same thing and Blair was giggling because his neck was ticklish.

It took a little while to solve the neck problem. Finally David took the shoestrings out of his good shoes and tied one around each of their necks—not quite tight enough to choke, but almost. That blocked the neck escape route, and the sleeves weren't a real problem.

"You can feel him climbing down your arm," David told Blair. "All you have to do is grab your arm, like this, when you feel him coming so he can't go any farther. Can you do that?"

Blair nodded. "But he tickles me. I'll laugh."

"Just pretend you're laughing at something else," David said. "Or else, just say you have a lizard in your shirt. Dad won't care. The only thing we're not supposed to tell is why we're doing it. That it's part of an initiation ordeal. Okay?"

"Okay," Blair said, giggling and squirming.

Amanda was waiting at the head of the stairs, and she checked everyone to be sure they had their reptiles. Breakfast went very smoothly except that Dad asked Blair once if something was wrong with him. When Blair shook his head, Dad said, "Well, sit still then and eat your breakfast. You're squirming all over your chair."

Blair was getting ready to say something, and he probably would have told Dad about his lizard, except that Janie interrupted with a long story about something or other.

A little later Molly asked about the shoestrings. Before David could explain their real purpose, Amanda said, "They're neckties. Like cowboy neckties."

"Oh," Molly said, "so you and Blair are cowboys today?"

David had to nod agreement, although actually he was embarrassed to have Dad and Molly think he'd do something as juvenile as playing cowboys.

He raised his eyebrows in a questioning way at Amanda, but she didn't seem to understand—even though David was sure that he'd made it clear that, while Dad had some definite prejudices about table manners, he didn't have any at all about reptiles. Amanda was really confusing. Just when it looked as if she was going to be doing everything she could to make the ordeals hard on everybody, she seemed to be doing the opposite. After breakfast David asked her about it.

"Why'd you make up that stuff about cowboys?" he asked. "I could have said we had pet snakes in our shirts. Dad wouldn't have cared. He wouldn't have made us get rid of them."

Amanda just looked at David for a while before she said, "Yes he would," and then she turned and walked away.

David was sure that Amanda didn't know what she was talking about. At least he was sure until about eleven o'clock, when he found out something that put everything in a different light. It started with a horrible scream from the kitchen.

David had been walking down the hall at the time and he turned and ran back. In the kitchen he found Janie standing near the sink and Molly backed into a corner near the stove.

"What's the matter?" David asked. "Who yelled?"

Molly was coming out of the corner slowly, with her eyes on Janie. "I'm sorry," she said. "That was foolish of me. But what is that awful thing?"

"It's just my salamander," Janie said. She turned to David. "I was just dampening him. I have to dampen him, or he'll die."

"A salamander?" Molly said, with a sick look on her face.

"Sure," Janie said. "I've had lots of pet ones. They won't hurt you, but you have to keep them wet or they die." She started towards Molly, opening her hand to show the freshly dampened salamander.

"Don't," Molly said, backing away.

"Take him outside, Janie," David said. "And don't dampen him in the sink anymore."

After Janie left, Molly came out of the corner and sat down, looking shaky. She smiled weakly at David.

"I'm sorry to be so silly, David," she said. "But I've always had

96

a terrible fear of anything like that. I was almost bitten by a rat-tlesnake once when I was a very little girl. My mother thought I had been bitten, and she got so hysterical she scared me about to death. Ever since then I've had a silly phobia about everything like that."

"You—you mean things like snakes and other reptiles?" David asked.

"Yes," Molly said, shivering. "Everything slimy and crawly. But snakes more than anything. Snakes are the worst."

"Oh, snakes are the worst," David repeated stupidly. He reached over and took hold of his right arm with his left hand, hoping that Molly wouldn't notice the wiggle going back up his right sleeve.

"Of course, I know most snakes are harmless," Molly said. "And I've really tried to get over being so silly about them, but they still frighten me almost out of my mind."

"Out of your mind?" David said. He was beginning to sound like an echo. He crossed his arms to hide the wiggle that was now going across his chest. As soon as it was out of sight behind him, he said, "But Amanda has a pet snake—and a pet horny toad."

Molly nodded, smiling in a strange way that seemed to mean the opposite of what a smile is supposed to mean. "I know," she said. "She certainly does."

"But don't you care?" David asked. "Why do you let her keep them?"

"Well, you see, it's difficult, David, because I didn't give them to her. Besides," Molly smiled a more normal smile, "they *are* in good strong cages. And I don't think Amanda ever takes them out."

"She doesn't take them out?" David asked. "Why not?"

But just then the kitchen door opened with a bang, and Amanda came in. "What's for lunch?" she said. "I'm hungry."

Chapter Nine

As soon as David found out about Molly's snake phobia, he began to see why Amanda had wanted to keep the reptiles a secret—or why she had wanted to keep them a secret at least until Dad was out of the house. One little scream out of Molly while Dad was around, and that would have been the end of the reptile ordeal—for everybody—forever. After thinking it over, David decided that there was only one thing for him to do—make very sure the rest of the reptiles were kept a secret from Molly, in spite of whatever Amanda might have in mind. To do that, the kids would have to be warned right away.

He found Janie and Esther in the yard and warned them and then went looking for Blair. It was a good thing he located Blair before Molly came upon him, because Blair was sitting on the landing playing with his lizard. He'd taken it out of his shirt and was letting it crawl around on the outside of his clothes.

"Hi," David said. "What are you doing?"

"I'm resting," Blair said.

"Resting?" David asked. "From what?"

"From the tickling."

"Oh. Well, you better not do it here. I've been looking for you to tell you something very important. Remember I said you could tell Dad and Molly about your lizard?"

Blair nodded.

"Well, you can't. I found out that Molly is scared to death of snakes and lizards. If she knew you had that lizard in your shirt, she'd probably faint."

Blair wrinkled his forehead. "Afraid of snakes," he said. "Amanda is afraid."

"No, Blair. Not Amanda. Molly! It's Molly who mustn't find out about the lizard in your shirt."

"Oh," Blair said, "Molly is afraid, too."

David sighed. It was really hard for Blair to get things straight sometimes. Blair held the lizard up to the banister and let it crawl along the wooden vine. It crawled up the vine to the cupid with the missing head.

"There's that cupid," Blair said. "Janie said a giant did it."

"No, it didn't," David said. "I told you before. Probably some kids who used to live here did it a long time ago. Probably some kid cut it off to try out his new saw, or something."

"No," Blair said. "A girl sawed it. A bad girl."

David grinned. Living with Janie, and now Amanda, it was no

wonder that Blair thought girls were the ones who caused trouble. He pulled the lizard down off the banister and handed it to Blair.

"You better put him back in your shirt," he said, "before Molly comes along and sees it. I'm going outside. Want to come?"

So everyone was warned in time to keep the reptile ordeal a secret, and the rest of the day went very smoothly. Most of the other ordeals went well, too. There were a few minor problems from time to time, but nothing too drastic.

During the ordeal where every neophyte had to wear a garlic bud and a slice of onion and a piece of anise weed on a string around his neck, there wasn't any real trouble. But David noticed Molly doing a lot of sniffing, and after dinner Dad asked David if he was remembering to bathe every day.

Then, on the day when no one was allowed to step on the wood floor, there were a few problems. The kitchen was easy, because it had linoleum, but all the rest of the house had hardwood floors and not a single room had wall-to-wall carpeting. It was pretty tricky, but by the end of the day they had established regular routes through most of the rooms. Coming into the living room from the hall, for instance, you stood on the edge of the hall runner and grabbed one of the living room double doors and swung hard enough to land on the little oriental throw rug in front of the love seat. Then you jumped to the hassock by Dad's chair and from there you slid on your stomach over the top of the grand piano and came down on the stack of TV floor cushions. Then you scooted along the edge of the library table on your seat and slid off onto the small rug at the other end of the room. From there you could just make it to the edge of the dining room rug. Nobody failed the ordeal that day, but a lamp got tipped over and a vase of flowers was broken, and Janie got caught right in the middle of the piano and was sent to her room as punishment for climbing on the furniture.

The only ordeal that anybody really failed was the day of silence. On that day no one could say anything unless he was asked a direct question and then he had to reply in only three words. Blair was the only one who made it through a whole day on the first try. David failed because Dad decided to have a serious man-to-man talk with him that evening after dinner. It was pretty discouraging because David had made it through the whole day until then, and he hated to have to ruin it at the last moment. But when he saw how upset Dad was, he knew he'd just have to fail, and try again on another day.

Dad was worried about a lot of things. He'd noticed a lot of strange behavior, he said, like bad table manners, and things getting broken, and basic rules of civilized behavior being ignored, such as not climbing on the furniture. And to top it all off, Dad said, after having to put up with a stepdaughter who hadn't been speaking to him for almost a month, he was beginning to get the feeling that his own children were developing the same malady.

"And just when I was hoping that you children would be on your very best behavior so Molly wouldn't be sorry she ever heard of the Stanley family."

David came very close to telling Dad the whole story that evening. All about the world of the occult and the ordeals and the initiation and everything. But just as he opened his mouth to start, he got a mental picture of Amanda's face, smiling her upside-down smile and saying something about "Davie tattling to his daddy."

So instead David just tried to reassure his father that it wasn't anything serious or permanent. "It must be just a phase we've been going through," he said. "You know how phases are."

Dad smiled. "I suppose so," he said. "But this one's been a little hard on Molly. I think Molly feels she hasn't been much of a success in her new job as mother of a big family."

"Wow," David said. "She shouldn't feel like that. We all think she's great. That is all of us but—"

"But who?" Dad asked.

"Well, I was thinking about Amanda."

"What about Amanda?"

David had talked himself into a hole. He was positive that Amanda wouldn't like him to mention what she had said about hating her mother. And David was sure Dad wouldn't like hearing it either. So he just said, "Well, Amanda would really rather live with her father, I guess. She really likes her father."

Dad made an angry noise. "Amanda has a lot to learn about liking—and loving," he said.

"Like what?" David asked.

Dad thought for a moment and then shook his head. "Well, what Amanda has to learn, and when, is not up to you and me, I guess. I guess we'd better stick to discussing our own problems. Or phases?"

David grinned. "Yeah, phases," he said. "That must be it. With moving to the country and getting a new mother and everything all at once, it's no wonder the kids have had a few phases to go through. But I think everything will be all right now. I think it's about all over." David could say it was over because the day of silence was the last ordeal and there was nothing left except the initiations. He couldn't see how that was going to cause trouble— or very much trouble anyway.

After that, it took about three more days before everyone had passed the day of silence ordeal, because David decided that only one person should try it at a time. That way it wasn't so noticeable. It worked fine. Under cover of Janie's chatter, no one noticed David's silence, and David tried hard to cover up for Janie. But that didn't work quite as well.

It would have taken a lot more distraction than David could provide to keep people from noticing something as unusual as a silent Janie. Dad and Molly kept asking her if something was wrong, and Janie kept saying "I feel bad" because that was all she could think of that only had three words in it. The result was that Janie got sent to bed and her temperature was taken. Later when David snuck her up a peanut butter sandwich, he was really worried about her. She seemed very tense and nervous, and her face was flushed. She didn't have any fever, though, and David decided it was just the strain of keeping quiet for so long. Sure enough, the next morning after Janie had talked steadily for almost three hours, she seemed to be entirely back to normal.

That was the end of the last ordeal, and there was nothing left

105

but the initiation. For several days Amanda spent a lot of time in her room with the door locked, getting things ready. She was very mysterious about the whole thing. When David asked her about it, she would just say that she was making preparations, and the rest of them had better be making their preparations.

Of course, by that she meant that David and the kids should be getting their robes ready, and they had been trying—but it wasn't easy.

Some of the requirements were not particularly difficult. For instance the rule that one of the things they wore had to have belonged to someone who was dead. David had helped Dad put some boxes of things that had been his mother's away in the attic. The clothing and jewelry in the boxes were things that Dad said Janie and Esther might like to have someday. So since Dad meant for the kids to have them someday, David figured he wouldn't mind too much if they used them a little right away.

On the other hand, however, Dad hadn't said that David could take anything out of the boxes yet, so it occurred to David that the things from the attic might fulfill another requirement. Maybe they could count for the articles that had to be stolen as well as the thing that belonged to a dead person. But when David suggested that the ring and the necklace and scarf and gloves from the box in the attic could count as stolen, Amanda looked scornful.

"Don't be silly," she said. "You have to steal from somebody alive."

David had been afraid of that—even before he asked. After he had thought about it some more he asked if flowers would be all right.

"Flowers?" Amanda said. "It has to be something you can wear, like clothing or jewelry."

"You can wear flowers. Like, in your buttonhole or hair. I was thinking those people down by where the road turns to go into the village have lots of flowers. They probably wouldn't even notice any were missing."

"It can't be flowers," Amanda said, "and besides, the thing that matters about stealing, is not whether anybody notices that anything is missing, but whether anybody sees you taking it."

"Yeah," David said. "I guess you're right." He just hadn't been thinking about it in that way.

"How did *you* do it?" he asked. "I mean, what part of your costume did you steal?"

"The black stockings," Amanda said. "I stole them at a rummage sale. Leah told me about its being easy to steal at a rummage sale because everything is such a mess and there're so many people around. I saw these black stockings on a big table with a lot of other junk, and I just put them in my pocket and walked out."

David decided that stockings would be a good thing to try for, for several reasons. The main thing was, of course, that stockings were small and easily hidden.

The only smaller thing to wear that David could think of was jewelry, and he'd already ruled that out, because of the kids. The thing was that, while David could understand that stealing something as part of an initiation was a lot different from just stealing for ordinary reasons, it might not be clear to kids as young as the twins, or even Janie. If he were to let them steal some jewelry for the initiation, and then, someday, one of them turned out to be a jewel thief, he knew he'd feel responsible.

That was the other good thing about stealing stockings. David had never heard of anybody taking up stocking robbery as a career.

However, having decided on stockings, there were still several problems to be solved. There were no clothing stores at Steven's Corners, and the only way for all the kids to get to the city would be for Molly to drive them there, and it wasn't likely she'd do that without knowing why they wanted to go. So the city was out.

That meant they had to do the stealing right there at home, which narrowed things down considerably. Actually, the only thing left to decide was whether it would be Molly's stockings or Dad's. Then, when David had gotten about that far in his planning, a wonderful opportunity presented itself.

Coming through the living room one morning, David noticed that Molly had left her mending basket near her favorite chair. It was a big basket, full of all sorts of torn and ripped stuff, because Molly didn't like mending and she was usually way behind on it. Near the top of the basket, David recognized the jeans he'd skinned the knee out of a couple of weeks before and the dress that Janie had gotten hung up by when she tried to jump the picket fence. Near the bottom of the basket David made a very interesting discovery.

Before they moved to the country, Dad had played tennis sometimes after his classes, but he'd had to give it up because of the time it took for the long commute home. So the large size white tennis socks at the bottom of Molly's basket had been there for some time. In fact, since Dad had quit tennis Molly would probably never get around to mending the socks, and Dad would never miss them. David looked around cautiously, lifted one sock out of the basket, leaving three others, and walked quietly back upstairs.

Then he found the kids and told them about his discovery and sent them down one at a time to steal a sock. Of course Janie wanted to be first, but David insisted that she be last. It was a good thing too, because she made such a production out of it, she almost gave the whole thing away. She crept down and back by such a complicated route and took so long about it, that Molly came out of her room where she'd been painting all morning, to make lunch while Janie was still sneaking around.

When Janie arrived upstairs a minute later, she was out of breath and there was something very strange about her appearance. She reached in her mouth and pulled out the tennis sock.

"Yick," she said, waving the sock in the air to dry it. "That was a close one. I almost had to swallow it."

Getting the tennis socks solved the hardest part of the initiation robes problems, except that the whole thing nearly turned out to be wasted. It wasn't until everyone had finished stealing a sock that David remembered that nothing could be white—and the socks were definitely white. David was very discouraged.

"Look," he told the kids. "We're going to have to do the whole stealing thing over again."

"Goody," Janie said. "I get to steal mine first this time."

"No, I mean we'll have to steal something else. The socks are white. Remember, nothing can be white?"

"Ohhh yeah," Janie said, holding up her sock and looking at it. Then all of a sudden her face lit up. "Hey, Tesser," she said, "where's Lopsided?"

Lopsided was a stuffed elephant that had been Esther's favorite toy until she got her vacuum cleaner. He was large and floppy and a deep dark red in color.

"Remember what happened to the sheets when Tesser put Lopsided in the wash with them?" Janie asked.

"Hey," David said, "yeah. Go get Lopsided, Tesser."

A few minutes later the socks were soaking in the wash basin along with Esther's elephant, and David was thinking that every once in a while Janie used her brains for something besides making a nuisance of herself.

The next day the tennis socks definitely weren't white, and everyone was ready for the initiation.

Chapter Ten

AMANDA HAD PICKED A TIME FOR THE INITIATION WHEN MOLLY WAS GOING to be away in the city all day. There was to be an opening at an art gallery where some of Molly's paintings were being shown, and Molly had promised to be there to help out. That left the whole day free and private for the initiation. David stayed awake a while the night before, thinking about it.

He didn't know exactly what he was expecting, but he felt strangely excited. He felt certain that something supernatural was about to happen. He went over in his mind all the things Amanda had told him about supernatural manifestations that had occurred while she and Leah were practicing magic—things like ghostly shapes appearing, mysterious voices being heard and people going into trances. David didn't know if he really expected something like that, but it didn't seem to matter. What did matter was his premonition that something fantastic was going to happen during the initiation.

Before Molly left that morning, she told everybody to be good and take care of things. She told Amanda to get the lunch and keep the house neat, and David to take care of the kids and keep them out of trouble.

"Why can't I take care of the kids and David get the lunch?" Amanda said.

"Well, I don't know," Molly said. "It's just that David has had a great deal of experience in taking care of them, but I suppose—"

"Never mind," Amanda interrupted. "I don't really want to take care of them. I just don't see why we couldn't arrange who does what ourselves without being told exactly what we have to do."

For a minute it looked as if Molly might be going to yell, or something, and David surprised himself by kind of wishing she would. But instead she caught her breath and bit her lip and got into her car.

As soon as she drove away, Amanda said, "Okay, let's get started. I hope you have your ceremonial robes all ready."

"They're ready," David said. "But it'll take us a while to get them on."

"It'll take me a while to get ready, too," Amanda said. "We'll meet in my room in about a half hour. Okay?" She turned to go upstairs, but then she stopped. "Hey," she said. "I need a dead lizard. Do you still have your lizard from the ordeal, Tesser?"

"I have him," Esther said, "but he's not a dead one." After the reptile ordeal everyone else had turned his reptile loose, but Esther had been keeping hers in a shoebox under her bed.

"You kill him and bring him along," Amanda said to David.

Suddenly David got mad. He didn't get mad very easily, and it always made it hard for him to talk. "Li—listen, Amanda," he said. "I'm not going to kill Tesser's lizard. Why don't you kill your horny toad if you need a dead reptile?"

Amanda glared at David. "I told you about that horny toad," she said. She turned to Esther. "Look, Tesser," she said, "nobody gave you that lizard as a gift or anything, and you can catch a million more just like him down in the creek bed. There's nothing special about that lizard."

Esther glared back at Amanda. "He thinks he's special," she said.

"Hey," Janie yelled so suddenly that everybody jumped. "Hey, I know where there's a—"

She started running out the door before she finished yelling so no one heard the last part of what she said, but in a minute she was back with something horrible between her thumb and forefinger. It was a *very* dead, very flat lizard.

"I saw him yesterday out on the road. Will he do?"

Amanda looked at the squashed lizard doubtfully.

"He's good and dead!" Janie said cheerfully, holding the lizard up towards Amanda.

Amanda turned away. "Okay," she said. "You go take him up and put him on the floor outside my door. I have a couple of things to do before I go up."

Janie gave the lizard to Esther. "Take it up to Amanda's room," she said. "Okay?"

Esther took it carefully in both hands, and Blair went over to look at it. As they both started off for the stairs, Esther said, "He's pretty dead, huh, Blair?"

"Dead," Blair said. "Can we fix him?"

"No," Esther said. "He's too dead."

"Can David?"

"Not David, even. He's too dead for David even."

Janie giggled. "Blair and Tesser think David can do anything," she said to Amanda. "Even fix dead things. Blair and Tesser are pretty dumb yet."

Amanda made her snorting noise, but then she stood looking after the twins for a long time with a funny look on her face.

Getting all the Stanleys into their ceremonial robes turned out to be even more hectic than David had expected. He'd been collecting all the stuff in a box in his closet, and he had everyone come into his room to dress, so he could be sure they didn't make any mistakes, but even so, things kept going wrong. Janie had a pouting spell because she wanted the necklace that had been their mother's, instead of the ring, and Blair and Esther kept losing their stolen socks because they were so much too big for their feet. Finally it was way past a half hour, and David was sure Amanda would be getting mad, so he rushed them into the last things, did a quick check to see if everybody had everything on the list, and pushed them all down the hall to Amanda's room.

When Amanda came to her door, she just stood staring at

them for a minute. Then she put her hand over her eyes, and took it away and stared at them some more. Then she put her hand back across her eyes and held it there for a minute, and when she took it away she said, "You're kidding."

"What do you mean, we're kidding?" David asked.

"Those aren't your ceremonial robes, are they?"

"Well, yes," David said. "What's wrong with them?" But while he was saying it, he suddenly knew. He'd been so busy putting all the little requirements on everybody that he hadn't paid much attention to the overall effect. And now when he thought about it, the overall effect of the Stanley kids' outfits wasn't too good, particularly when you compared it to the way Amanda looked.

Amanda was wearing the long slinky black dress that came almost down to her ankles. Below the dress you could see her special ceremonial shoes, high topped old ladies' shoes, made of cracked and peeling patent leather. Around her neck on a leather thong was a magic medalion. Her hair was braided and looped; the shiny triangle shone on her forehead; and draped over everything like gaudy wings, was the shimmery purplish-red shawl. Anyone looking at Amanda, even if he'd never seen her before, would immediately think of things like cloudy, moon-haunted nights, low chanting voices and bubbling cauldrons.

On the other hand, looking at the Stanley kids in their ceremonial costumes didn't make you think of anything in particular. Of course the difference was that David hadn't been able to spend a lot of time going through junk shops and attending rummage sales. He'd had to depend on just what he could find in the rag bag and a couple of boxes of old stuff in the attic. All of it fit the rules, David had seen to that. All of it was fairly old, none of it was white, and each one of the kids had one thing that had belonged to a dead person, and one stolen sock. It was just the general overall appearance that wasn't right. For instance, there was something particularly wrong with the way Blair looked.

Blair was wearing a sweatshirt that Dad had worn in college, so obviously it was very old. It was a faded blue color except for the yellow letters that said University of California across the front. It bagged a lot on Blair, except where the tightly knit waist pulled it in fairly close, just below his knees. David had rolled the sleeves way up, into big fat doughnuts of cloth, to get them short enough to let the tips of Blair's fingers hang out. For his article that had belonged to a dead person, David had tied a scarf that had been their mother's around Blair's neck like a necktie. The scarf was pink and filmy and so long that Blair stepped on the ends now and then when he tried to walk. He had a fuzzy slipper on one foot, and on the other was the stolen sock, a dirty pink now and tied around the ankle with one of Esther's hair ribbons to keep it from falling off.

Looking at Blair, really looking at the overall picture for the first time, David couldn't help smiling.

"He does look a little weird," he said to Amanda.

Amanda snorted. "Weird?" she said. "No, he doesn't look weird. That's just it. He ought to look weird, and all he looks is ridiculous. All of you do."

David had to admit she was right. All of the Stanleys looked pretty ridiculous, with odds and ends of rag bag stuff and baggy pink tennis socks on one foot.

"Come on," David said to the kids and started back towards his room.

"Wait a minute," Amanda yelled. "Where do you think you're going?"

"To get out of this junk," David said, feeling more ridiculous—and angrier—every minute.

Amanda snorted. "Come back here. I never said it wouldn't do. I just said it looked funny. You'll have to do, because there's no telling when we'll have another private day without any adults around."

David almost didn't go back. He almost went into his room and locked the door, but he didn't. He went back, but it wasn't because Amanda had said they would *do*. He went back because he suddenly remembered about his premonition, and he knew he had to. Something was going to happen, and he had to find out what—ridiculous or not.

As they went in the door to Amanda's room, Esther pulled on his hand.

"We do *too* look weird," she said. "Don't we, David?"

Chapter Eleven

IN AMANDA'S ROOM EVERYTHING WAS READY FOR THE INITIATION. THE blinds were pulled and blankets hung over the blinds to shut out the slightest glow of light. Walking through the door was like walking out of a bright morning into midnight. Only a faint flicker of candlelight glowed in the center of the room, leaving the corners in deep shadow.

Moving forward, David could see that the light came from a candle burning under a metal frame on which sat a small round kettle. When everyone was in the room, Amanda closed the door, walked to the opposite side of the room, turned slowly and faced David and the kids.

"Will the neophytes be seated around the cauldron," she said in a solemn high-pitched voice.

Esther, who was still hanging onto David's hand, began to tug on it.

"Cauldron," David whispered out of the corner of his mouth, pointing at the kettle.

"Oh," Esther whispered. She turned around to Blair and said, "That's it, Blair. That's a cauldron."

"Shhh," David hissed. Putting one hand over Esther's mouth and the other on top of her head, he shoved her down onto the floor. Then he showed Blair where to sit, next to Esther.

"*Sit down around the cauldron,*" Amanda repeated, and David turned in time to see Janie tiptoeing up to peek in the kettle. He grabbed her by the back of her robe and pulled her back to her place in the circle. When everyone was finally seated, Amanda got a large roll of paper from her desk and brought it back to the circle.

"First," she said, "every neophyte must be given a new name. A spiritual name."

Janie got to be first. She sat cross-legged with her eyes closed while Amanda spread out the roll of paper in front of her. David could see that words had been written here and there at different angles, all over the paper.

"Touch the paper with your finger and the name you touch will be your new name," Amanda said. "Keep your eyes closed."

"What if I don't like it?" Janie said.

"Touch the paper."

Janie leaned forward, and David was pretty sure she was peeking from under her long eyelashes. Finally she put her finger down exactly in the middle of one of the words.

Amanda picked up the paper. "Calla," she said. "The spirits have given you Calla as your new name."

Janie smiled. "I like it," she said.

David was next, and his finger lit on the word Templar. It didn't seem like much of a name to him, but he liked the sound of it pretty well.

Blair was next and without peeking he put his finger down at the beginning of a short word that turned out to be Star.

"Hey," David said. "That's good. That's a good name for Blair."

"The spirits don't make mistakes," Amanda said.

Esther was next, but when Amanda put the paper down in front of her, she put her hands behind her back and wouldn't take them out.

"I'm Tesser," she said. "I don't want to be anybody else."

Everyone argued and scolded, but it didn't do any good. Esther was that way. She didn't have too many opinions, but when she had one, there was no use trying to change it.

"Look," David said to Amanda. "Remember you said once you thought Tesser was her spiritual name. Maybe it is. Maybe that's why she started calling herself that. Why can't her spiritual name be Tesser?"

Amanda shrugged. "All right," she said. "It's all right with me. But if it's the wrong name she'll never get very far in the occult world." She looked down at Esther, sitting solid and stubborn with her hands behind her. "Not that she would anyway," Amanda said.

As soon as everyone had his name chosen, Amanda put a record on her record player. It was weird music, oriental David decided, with high pitched wailing instruments and soft deep drums that thudded monotonously, like giant heartbeats. Then she lit some incense sticks and put them in holders in the four corners of the room. When that was done, she disappeared behind the curtain that hung over the closet doorway. The light came on behind the curtain, and Amanda stayed there for several minutes.

In the bedroom the dark air was becoming sweet and smoky, from the burning incense. The strange music droned on and on, and the Stanleys went on sitting cross-legged around the cauldron waiting for Amanda to reappear. At last the light went off in the closet, and Amanda came out, walking slowly and ceremoniously and carrying at arm's length a small metal box. She began to walk around and around the cauldron, holding the box out in front of her and chanting some strange words. The words were something like, "malu—arabon—ralu—belabor."

The walking and the chanting went on and on, and David found himself swaying in a slow circle in time with Amanda's progress around the cauldron. The dim flickering light, Amanda's slowly swaying step, the wailing, throbbing music, the heavy sweetness of the incense, the occasional flash of reflected light from the triangle on Amanda's forehead—all of it—began to blend and swirl in David's mind. He was beginning to feel very strange; his head felt light and dizzy and there were some strange sensations right around his stomach. He was wondering vaguely, with a strange detached kind of excitement, if he were beginning to go into a trance, when a loud voice said, "You better stop that, Amanda."

It was Esther. Everyone looked at her. Even Amanda stopped her stately progress around the cauldron and looked at Esther.

"You better stop that before you throw up. When I ran around and around the coffee table, I threw up. Didn't I David."

"Shhh!" David said, shaking his head at her.

"I did, too," Esther said. "All over the Indian rug and clear out the door. Don't you remember?"

"Shhh!" everyone said so fiercely that Esther looked startled.

"I did. I did, too," she whispered stubbornly, but her face crinkled, on the edge of crying.

Amanda went on walking around the table, and Esther was quiet except for a few sniffs. After one or two more times around, Amanda stopped and stood still, holding the metal box out over the cauldron with one hand. With the other hand she reached into the box and took something out. She held the object—it looked like a few dead twigs—out over the cauldron and repeated the chant, "Malu—arabon—ralu—belabor." Then she dropped the twigs into the steaming kettle.

She walked around the cauldron once more and stopped again, to drop something else into the brew. This time it looked like a few long strands of hair. The next time around it was a dead flower, and after that came what seemed to be a piece of bone, a feather, a dried mushroom, and a small white object that looked like somebody's tooth.

David was fascinated, and the kids were, too. They sat perfectly still, without so much as twitching, while Amanda went around the cauldron, dropping the strange objects into her magic brew. Finally she stopped and held the box out again with both hands, over the cauldron. In the same singsong voice she used to say the

chant, she asked, "Would one of the neophytes stand and approach the sacred fire?"

Of course, Janie got there first. She bounced to her feet and then took two slow solemn steps to face Amanda across the cauldron.

"Neophyte Calla," Amanda chanted. "You may add the next magic ingredient to the cauldron."

She held the box down, and Janie raised her arm slowly and stiffly and lowered her hand into the box. She wiggled her fingers for a moment and then raised her hand, holding the squashed lizard with the tips of her fingers. Amanda stepped back and Janie held the lizard over the kettle.

"Add the ingredient to the cauldron," Amanda said again.

But instead Janie started walking around the kettle just as Amanda had been doing. She walked slowly and solemnly with the squashed lizard held at arms length in front of her. She was holding her chin very high and letting her long eyelashes droop mysteriously over her eyes. The second time around the kettle she began to chant. The words weren't quite the same as the ones in Amanda's chant, but they were very similar. Right after the chant, Janie added a sway in time to the music. As she walked she swayed, far to one side and then far to the other, waving the squashed lizard in front of her with every sway.

David glanced at Amanda. She had stepped back out of the way and was just standing there with her hands on her hips. About then Janie began to dance. She made a little tiptoeing run from one end of the room to the other and ended with a graceful leap, twirling the lizard around her head.

"Stop!" Amanda shrieked, and Janie, who had just started another glide, stopped in mid-leap and stared at Amanda.

"Neophyte Calla," Amanda said between clenched teeth. "*Put the magic ingredient in the cauldron!*"

Janie sighed, shrugged, dropped the lizard in the pot, and plopped down in her place on the floor.

After a minute, Amanda sat down on the floor, too. "The next part of the initiation ceremony will be the sacrifice," she announced.

"What do we sacrifice?" David asked.

"The object to be sacrificed must be one of your most treasured possessions. It must be something of great value. Each of you will be excused one at a time to go and find a sacrifice and bring it back. Then the ceremony will begin."

Amanda stood by the door while each of the Stanleys went out, one by one, and came back with a sacrifice. David picked out his six bladed jackknife, and it seemed to be the right kind of thing because Amanda nodded when she saw it and put it in the metal box. However Esther got sent back once to change hers and Janie twice. David wondered what they had picked.

Finally each one's sacrifice was in the metal box, and Amanda had them all take their places on the floor again and blindfolded them. David's blindfold was a large silk scarf, and Amanda tied it so tight that it felt as if his eyes were being pushed back into his head. When everyone was blindfolded, Amanda gave each one back his own sacrifice to hold, until the spirits arrived. With her voice coming from her spot in the circle, she explained that she was blindfolding herself and that soon the spirits would arrive to accept the sacrifices. The neophytes, she said, were to hold their offerings up high over their heads, and when they felt something touch their hands they were to drop their offering into the metal box.

"Who'll be holding the box?" Janie asked.

"The spirits," Amanda said.

"Where will you be," Janie asked.

"Right here on the floor," Amanda answered. "I'm blindfolded, too."

"Oh," Janie said.

Except for the wail of the music, the room became very quiet. Behind the tight blindfold David's eyes were getting more and more uncomfortable. The arm that held his jackknife above his head was getting numb and achy, too. At last something touched his wrist, and he felt the metal box under his hand. As he put the knife into the box, he listened carefully for the sound of feet moving on the carpet in front of him, but he didn't hear a thing. A minute later, however, he heard a slight sound from where Janie was sitting, on his right.

Then Janie's voice whispered, "Do I get it back after the initiation?" There was no answer, and Janie whispered a little louder. "Spirits! Do I get it back?"

There was no other sound, and after what seemed a very long

while Amanda's voice came from her side of the circle. "The sacrifice is over. The neophytes may remove their blindfolds."

When David got his blindfold off, he couldn't see anything for a few seconds because his eyes had been so squashed, but as soon as his sight returned, the first thing he noticed was the metal box sitting on the floor near the cauldron. It was empty.

"The sacrifices have been accepted," Amanda said. "That means you have all been accepted into the world of the occult. We are now ready for the anointing."

The anointing was the last part of the initiation ceremony and the shortest. It consisted of each one of the neophytes approaching the cauldron where Amanda waited, holding a thin white bone that looked as if it might at one time have been a part of a turkey's leg. In front of the cauldron, they knelt and Amanda dipped the bone into the kettle and then touched it to their foreheads and the palms of their hands. That was all there was to it.

David felt vaguely disappointed. During the anointing he tried to get back into the spirit of the occasion, but he wasn't able to. He tried to recapture the excited trancelike feeling that he'd experienced earlier in the ceremony—but it wouldn't come back. While Amanda chanted solemnly and touched the white bone to his face and hands the only sensation he got was a slightly gaggy feeling, because the steam from the cauldron was coming up right in his face and it really smelled like the devil.

As they were getting ready to leave the room, Amanda said, "Well, you're all wizards now and members of the occult world.

But you still have a lot of things to learn yet, of course. You all have to decide what you'd like to study next."

"I'd like to learn about seances and summoning spirits," David said.

"No," Esther said. "Let's learn about making rabbits, first."

"Can I get my ring back now, Amanda?" Janie asked.

It took a minute for Janie's question to register with David, but when it did he grabbed her hand. Sure enough, the real pearl and fire opal ring that had been their mother's, and that Janie had been wearing as a part of her ceremonial robes, was missing.

"Did you use Mom's ring as a sacrifice?" David demanded, and when Janie nodded, he grabbed her and shook her. "You can't do that. It was Mom's, and you can't give it away. You were supposed to keep it to remember her by when you're grown up. I only let you wear it for the ceremony because you promised to take good care of it."

David was really angry at Janie, and she knew it because, for once instead of arguing, she only stared at him with tears filling up her eyes.

"But I couldn't find anything else that was all right," she said finally. "But I'll get it back. I'll get it back again."

David turned to Amanda. "She has to have the ring back," he said. "It was Mom's. She wasn't really supposed to have it until she was older and could take better care of it. I shouldn't have even let her wear it."

But Amanda only looked at David with stony eyes. "I can't give it back," she said. "She sacrificed it. It belongs to the spirits now."

128

"Look, Amanda," David said, "I'm not kidding—"

Before he could say any more, Amanda whirled on him in a screaming explosion. "What do you mean—kidding?" she shrieked. "Do you think I've just been kidding about the supernatural? If that's what you think, you can just get out of here. Get out!"

Afterwards David wasn't sure whether Amanda had really pushed anybody physically, or only with her voice, but in a second or two all the Stanleys were in the hall.

"Look, Amanda," David said, "I didn't mean—"

"Yeah, well, what did you mean? What did you mean?"

"He just meant I can't give my mother's ring away," Janie said in a quavering voice. "I have to get it back. I just have to."

Amanda stared from one of them to the other breathing hard. "Well," she said finally, "well—"

But just then Blair came out of Amanda's room. David was surprised because he was sure Blair had been pushed out with the rest of them. But apparently he'd gone back in while they were busy talking. Everyone was surprised to see Blair coming through the door, but they were even more surprised when they saw what was in his outstretched hand. It was the pearl and opal ring.

Esther squealed with excitement, and everyone else gasped. Janie grabbed the ring away from Blair and put it on. Amanda was looking at Blair with such angry eyes that David started to step in between them.

"Where did you get that?" Amanda said, and there wasn't a bit of her usual cool in her voice.

"There," Blair said, pointing, "behind the curtain."

129

"You were peeking."

"No," Blair said. "I didn't peek."

"Oh yeah! How did you find it then?"

Blair's lips moved, but no sound came out.

"Something told him," Esther said. "Something tells Blair lots of things."

"You're lying," Amanda yelled at Blair. She turned to David. "That crazy kid is lying."

David felt his face getting hot, and he knew he was going to stutter, but he didn't care. Blair was different, but he wasn't crazy and Amanda couldn't say he was.

"Sh-sh-shut up!" he yelled at Amanda, and grabbing Blair's arm and Esther's shoulder he marched them down the hall to his room. Behind him he heard Amanda slam her door so hard the whole house seemed to shake.

At first, for quite a while, David was just angry, but when he began to cool off he began to feel very disappointed. He'd been so sure that something—well, different—was going to happen. He really hadn't realized how much he'd been counting on it. He still didn't know exactly what he'd expected, but he did know it hadn't happened.

Of course there had been the spirits who came to take the sacrifices—at least, according to Amanda, there had been spirits. But whatever had held the metal box, David knew it hadn't been what he'd been hoping for.

Sometime later, when David got around to wondering *why* his premonition had fizzled, he had an uncomfortable thought. It occurred to him that it was probably his own fault—his and the kids. Because, on the whole, it was pretty obvious that none of the Stanleys had much talent for the kind of magic Amanda was trying to do.

Chapter Twelve

As usual, David didn't have the slightest idea about what to expect next from Amanda. By the next day he wasn't angry any longer, himself—he didn't really think Amanda had meant what she said about Blair. But he didn't have a clue as to how Amanda was feeling.

He needn't have worried. The next morning Amanda was the friendliest he'd ever seen her. She even knocked on the door of David and Blair's room and came in and talked to them, and she'd certainly never done that before.

First she looked at the books in David's bookcase, and then she said hello to Blair, who was just waking up. Then, while David was getting out some clothes for Blair, Amanda sat down on the foot of the bed and said, "Well, we better get started on making plans for the seance."

"The seance?" David said, surprised. "Well, okay. I thought that maybe after what happened yesterday and—"

Amanda shrugged. She turned her eyes slowly to David's and held them there—blank and cool. "What happened?" she said, and the way she said it meant that it was ridiculous to even mention it. Then she started telling David and Blair about some seances she had attended, and one in particular that Leah and some of her friends had arranged. During that seance they had summoned the spirit of a girl who had died in the room where the seance was being held, many years before. She was telling how the girl's voice had come from a white mist in the corner of the room, when Molly called to say that breakfast was ready.

At breakfast Dad reminded everyone that he was leaving the next day on the three-week field trip, and that they had all promised to be responsible and civilized while he was gone. While Dad was talking, David was wondering what Dad would think about the seance they were planning. It wasn't that he thought he ought to get permission. He had just never discussed seances with Dad, and he was curious about what Dad would say. He wondered what he'd say about trying to talk to someone who was dead. David really thought about bringing the subject up, but somehow he never got around to it.

So the next morning Dad packed his gear and left, and for a couple of days things went quite smoothly. Molly painted a lot of the time, and David and Amanda did a lot of talking and reading about seances. Then on about the third day, the electrical system of Westerly House, which had always been a little tricky, really started to fall apart.

First, sparks started flying every time the living room switch was turned on, and then Molly noticed that when she plugged in the iron, the TV turned into nothing but static. Molly was pretty calm about the whole thing, until she got a shock from the kitchen faucet; then she began to get really nervous. When David heard her talking to the real estate man on the telephone, she sounded a little bit hysterical.

"No," she was saying, "I don't think we can wait until someone can come out from the city. The house could catch on fire any moment—if it doesn't explode first. Isn't there someone around Steven's Corners who understands about electricity?"

After a while she calmed down enough to listen for a minute, and when she finally hung up, she seemed to be feeling better. She looked a little embarrassed when she realized that David was still in the room and had heard her conversation.

"Oh, David," she said, "I didn't know you were here. I hope I didn't scare you. I'm sure it's not as serious as I made it sound. It's just that sneaky invisible things like electricity have always given me the creeps. And wouldn't you know it would wait until your father left to act up."

"Yeah," David said. "Dad's pretty good at fixing things like that."

"I know he is," Molly said. "But this just can't wait for him to get home. Mr. Ballard at the real estate office is going to call an old man who lives down at the Corners. His name is Mr. Golanski, and he's retired now; but he's done all kinds of building work, and he should be able to find out what's gone wrong."

Molly was trying to be very relaxed and reassuring; but David could tell she was still worried, because she insisted that all the kids go outside until the repairman got there. The little kids didn't notice, because they usually played outside anyway, but Amanda, who spent most of her time in her room, was very sarcastic.

"Wow," she said to David, loud enough for her mother to hear. "Talk about hitting the panic button over nothing. Fire drill time! Abandon ship!"

As she went past the living room, Amanda reached inside the door and flipped the switch with a bored expression on her face. This time the crackling noise was louder, sparks flew out, and a curl of black smoke drifted into the room. Molly made a little yelping noise, and even Amanda stopped looking bored and walked a little faster towards the front door.

The kids were playing in the front yard, and David and Amanda were sitting on the porch steps, when an old wreck of a pickup truck turned into the driveway. The man who got out of the truck had white hair and his skin was wrinkled into deep gullies down his cheeks, but his eyes were dark and bright and he moved in a strong firm way. He took a huge wooden tool chest and a big hammer out of the back of the truck and started towards the front door. Watching him trudging along with his white hair bushing around his head and his tools in his hands, David suddenly pictured a whole procession of identical old men marching along a tunnel, singing a deep thundering song.

"He looks like some kind of troll," he whispered to Amanda.

Amanda smiled her downward smile. "Yeah," she said, "what a face."

The old man reached the steps and stood looking at them for a moment without saying anything. He looked from David to Amanda and then back again. Finally he said, "Rom Golanski. Where's the mischief?"

The front door opened just then, and Molly came out.

"Mr. Golanski?" she asked. When the old man nodded slowly, she said, "Oh, I'm so glad to see you, Mr. Golanski. I'm Mrs. Stanley. My husband is away, and the whole house seems to be going to pieces."

Molly ushered Mr. Golanski into the house, and David and Amanda could hear her explaining about the problem as she went down the hall. Amanda put her head down on her knees and stayed that way for a long time.

The morning went by slowly. Mr. Golanski was in and out of the house, tearing wires out of walls and banging and hammering. Molly didn't shut herself in her studio to paint, so there was no chance to do anything about the seance. Amanda spent most of the morning on the porch swing with a book, and David wandered around doing not much of anything. Finally he asked Mr. Golanski if he could help.

Mr. Golanski straightened up from where he was pulling a wire through a hole in a baseboard and gave David a long dark look.

"Help?" he asked.

"Yes," David said. "I was wondering if there was anything I could do."

"That depends. Yes, I think that depends on what you've done already."

David wondered if the old man might be a little bit crazy. Or was it just his way of asking if David had had any experience in electrical work? David explained that he hadn't done much work with electricity, but that he just thought he might help by carrying tools and holding things.

Mr. Golanski went on staring for a long time before he said, "Yes, I see. I see. Well now, I'm going upstairs next, and you might gather up those tools and that roll of wire near the door and carry them up there."

So David was right behind Mr. Golanski, all loaded down with tools and wire, when they got to the foot of the stairs—and stopped. Mr. Golanski put his hand on the first newel post, on the ball held by the first two cupids, and stood still looking up and down and up and down the stairs. David waited until his arms began to get tired, and then he tried to edge past to go on up.

"I'll just take these things on up—" he said, but Mr. Golanski put out his arm so David couldn't get by.

"My father's work," he said. "This banister was carved by my father when I was a very small boy."

"Your father?" David said. "Wow! He must have been a great carver. My dad says they're really great banisters. He says he's never seen anything like them in this country."

Just then Amanda came in the front door carrying her book, and David told her about Mr. Golanski's father and the banisters.

Amanda stopped to listen, looking bored as usual, and Mr. Golanski went on telling how his father had come to America to get land and be a farmer because there wasn't much work anymore for woodcarvers, which is what he was. Then he had met Mr. Westerly and Mr. Westerly had brought him and his family to Steven's Corners and helped him find land and a job. And when Mr. Westerly started building his new house, Mr. Golanski's father had carved the banisters to show his appreciation.

"Wow," David said. "That was really a great thing for him to do. These banisters are really a work of art. That's what my dad says."

"Yes," Mr. Golanski said. "A work of art. True. But they are in need of refinishing. Someday I will come back and do that. You may tell your father that I will come. I will make them like new again. Except for the cherub on the landing who was damaged by the poltergeist. I cannot replace the head."

David would hardly have paid any attention to the word "poltergeist" because he'd never heard it before; but the moment Mr. Golanski said it Amanda snapped to attention as if he'd just fired off a cannon.

"Poltergeist?" she said. "What poltergeist?"

Mr. Golanski gave her his long dark look. "Ah," he said. "You know about poltergeist, then? Yes, I am not surprised."

"What about a poltergeist, Mr. Golanski?" Amanda said in an unnaturally polite and eager voice. "Was there a poltergeist in this house once?"

"Yes. Yes, there was. It was only a short time after the banisters were finished. A great fuss it was—in all the papers for weeks. With the village full of policemen and professors."

"Was there—were there any children living here then?" Amanda asked. "Were there any boys or girls in the house then?"

Mr. Golanski turned away from where he had been inspecting a crackled place in the varnish on the banisters and looked again for a long time at Amanda before he answered. Then he said, "Yes, you know a great deal about such things. You know too much, perhaps." Then he turned and motioning to David to follow, he went on up the stairs. Amanda followed close behind.

When Mr. Golanski had started to take apart the switch in the upstairs hall, she began to ask some more questions. She asked about the children who had lived in Westerly House and what kinds of things had happened, but she didn't get any more answers. It was almost as if Mr. Golanski had suddenly gone deaf. Only once when she asked about the cupid without the head, he stopped working and turned toward her.

"Ahh," he said. "The cupid. It was cut off one night when there was much damage and disturbance in the house. The Westerlys wanted my father to carve another head to replace it, but he refused. He felt it would be better if they found the missing head. He felt sure it could be found."

By that time David was getting wild with curiosity, and it was obvious that Amanda was, too; but Mr. Golanski refused to say anymore. Amanda kept trying, asking all sorts of questions, until Mr. Golanski finally whirled around at her with his bushy white eyebrows drawn together and his wrinkles drawn into angry gulches up and down his face. He waved his arm at her fiercely and said, "Go now. I am busy," and Amanda went.

David was holding the end of a measuring tape for Mr. Golanski or he would have gone too. He did go soon afterwards, and in the meantime he didn't ask any more questions. When he finally got away, Amanda was waiting for him on the front porch.

She was looking so excited and enthusiastic that, for a second, David hardly recognized her.

"Isn't that fantastic," she said. "A poltergeist, right here in this house."

"Look," David said, "would you mind telling me what a poltergeist is? I mean exactly. I have a general idea but—"

But Amanda wasn't paying any attention to him at all. She went right on talking almost as if she were talking to herself.

"That means this is a real haunted house. Probably even a famous haunted house—or at least it was once."

"It's some kind of a ghost, isn't it?" David went on asking. "But why is it called a 'poltergeist'?"

All of a sudden Amanda seemed to notice him.

"Don't you know what a poltergeist is?" she asked. "It's a ghost, but it's a particular kind of ghost. *Polter* means noisy, and *geist* means spirit. So poltergeist means noisy ghost. There've been a lot of very famous ones. They've been studied by scientists and detectives and people like that!"

"How do you know all that?" David asked.

"Oh, I've read about them lots of times, and Leah knows all

about them, too." Amanda thought for a while before she went on slowly, as if she were trying to remember. "They always make lots of noise and throw things. Rocks usually but other stuff, too. They move things around when no one is near them, and they play tricks on people. And there's another strange thing about them."

"What's that?" David asked.

"When they appear it's almost always in a house where there are children of a certain age."

"What age?" David asked.

Amanda turned towards him but she didn't seem to be looking at him. "About my age," she said.

Chapter Thirteen

THE NEXT MORNING WHEN MOLLY MADE A QUICK TRIP INTO THE CITY TO deliver some paintings, Amanda went with her. When Molly came back, she was alone.

"Where's Amanda?" David asked.

"At the library," Molly said. "She's going to come home on the bus."

"Still at the library?" David asked. "I thought she was going there this morning."

"She did. But when I went to pick her up, she insisted she had to stay longer; so we found out about bus connections, and she's going to catch the 2:00 bus. It comes through Steven's Corners about 3:00."

Before she left that morning Amanda had told David she was going to the library to do research on poltergeists. There hadn't been much time to discuss it, and all morning David had been wondering what she thought she was going to find out, because it seemed to him that she already knew everything there was to know about poltergeists. The more he thought about it, the more curious he got; and by afternoon he decided to walk down to the bus stop to meet her.

The bus stop at Steven's Corners was on the other side of the village where the city road came through. It was quite a long way, particularly in the afternoon heat of a dusty August day. By the time David got to the little three-sided bus stop shelter, his face was damp with sweat and gritty with dust. He was sitting there feeling very tired and hot when the bus pulled up and Amanda got off, looking extremely cool. Of course the bus was air-conditioned, but Amanda's cool was the kind that said that she hadn't noticed that people on the bus were staring at her far-out rummage store outfit and the Center-of-Power triangle on her forehead. Amanda's expression said that she didn't have any idea people were staring, and even if she did, it would only bore her. She went on looking bored until the bus pulled away and she noticed David.

"David," she said, rushing over to him, "wait till you hear what I found out."

"About poltergeists?" David asked.

"About the poltergeist. The one that was in Westerly House."

"How did you do that?"

"Well, I remembered that the house was built in 1895, and the old man said the poltergeist started not long after the house was built. So I asked to see the files of all the old local newspapers starting with 1895. They weren't going to let me because I'm not an adult, but finally they did, after I told them it was for a summer school project. Only they kept snooping to see that I didn't cut out anything. But I found it finally, starting in September of 1896."

On the way back to the house David didn't even notice the heat and the dust, because Amanda was telling him a fantastic story about what had happened in Westerly House. The two old ladies who had lived in the house until just a few months before the Stanleys had bought it were young girls at the time, just twelve and fourteen years old. Their names were Mabel and Harriette, and before they came to Steven's Corners, they had lived all over the world. Their father, Mr. Westerly, had worked for the government and had been sent to all different countries. But then he had come to Steven's Corners to retire and be a farmer; and not long after the family moved in, the trouble had started.

At first it was mostly rocks. Rocks and pebbles were thrown all around the house and yard—sometimes one or two at a time, and sometimes almost in showers. Then there began to be noises at night, and large pieces of furniture would be moved all around the house. The police were called in when things began to be broken, vases and lamps and window panes. One newspaper had an interview with a maid who lived in the house at the time, and who claimed to have seen a large cut-glass lamp pick itself up and dash itself to pieces on the opposite wall of the room. There were accounts in the papers about special investigators, and even a couple of professors from a university, who had come to Steven's Corners to study the strange happenings at Westerly House.

Daily Journal

STEVEN'S CORNERS SINCE 1861

SEPTEMBER 14, 1896

Ghostly Doings Westerly House

[body text illegible]

Where Is Cupid's Head?

[body text illegible]

Storms Damage Midwestern Towns

[body text illegible]

Engaged

[body text illegible]

Utah Nine Months Old As A State

[body text illegible]

Jone's Copper Weather Vanes

"Did they ever solve it?" David asked. "I mean, did they ever find out who was doing it?"

"No." Amanda said. "No, they never found out. There was an article in the paper by one of the professors, who claimed that Harriette, the oldest Westerly girl, was probably responsible, but he didn't have any proof at all. They did find out that the things only happened when the girls were in the house, but that doesn't mean they did them. The spirit had to have a person to take power from, and that person happened to be Harriette. One time, the time the front window was broken and the cupid's head was chopped off, Harriette was in bed in her room asleep with three people watching her when it happened. So that was proof that she didn't do it."

"What did they do then?"

"Well, then the mother sent for a famous medium, a person who calls up spirits, to come to the house. And the woman came and said that the house had an evil spirit in it and there would have to be a special ceremony to get rid of it. But the father, Mr. Westerly, sent the girls away to a boarding school, and everything stopped. So they never had the ceremony after all."

"Wow!" David said. "I wonder why they didn't tell us all that stuff before we bought the house. They probably thought we'd be afraid to buy it."

"Or else they just didn't know about it," Amanda said. "It happened such a long time ago, and most of the people who knew about it have probably already died or moved away."

"I wish Dad were here," David said.

"Why?" Amanda asked.

146

"Because he'd really be interested. I mean it was practically an historical event—in the papers and everything. And right in our own house."

Amanda had stopped walking and was looking at David. All she said was "Davie!" but the way she said it and the look told him exactly what she meant.

"Look, Amanda," he said, "I don't get it. I don't see why I can't tell my dad about this. He'd really be interested, and it's not as if it were some big secret. I mean, it was in the papers and everyone knew about it."

"Everybody knew about it *then*. But not now."

"You mean you're not even going to tell Molly?"

"Tell Molly! Are you crazy? You know what a chicken she is. She'd probably refuse to stay in the house another night."

David hadn't thought of that possibility. Under the circumstances, it was probably best if he didn't tell Dad or Molly, but it really was too bad. It was such a great thing to tell, and now there was no one to tell it to except the kids, and they were too young to appreciate it.

As soon as they got back to Westerly House, Amanda shut herself in her room and stayed there that night and most of the next day except at mealtime. David was dying to talk to her, and once or twice he even knocked on her door, but she only yelled at him to go away because she was busy. It was very frustrating.

The more David thought about the poltergeist, and the things Amanda had told him about it, the more interesting ideas and questions kept coming to his mind.

He wanted to know which rooms the rocks fell in, and which wall the lamp had smashed against. And which room had been Harriette's room, where she lay asleep with people watching her while the poltergeist banged through the downstairs part of the house, breaking windows and chopping off the head of the cupid.

He wondered if it could have been his room. The very room he was sitting in. He got up and walked around trying to picture it the way it might have been then: where Harriette's bed had been, probably an old-fashioned bed with a canopy on top, and where the watchers sat, and what they had done when the noises started downstairs, slowly and softly maybe at first, and then louder and *louder*—

Just at that moment there was a bang from somewhere nearby, and David jumped about a foot before he realized the sound had come from the girls' room. It was probably only Janie having a tantrum about something. He started down the hall to tell her to stop, but on the way he knocked again on Amanda's door. The only answer was a voice saying, "Go away. I'm thinking."

Chapter Fourteen

It wasn't until late in the afternoon that Amanda finally came out of her room. The kids were running around the lawn in their bathing suits, and David was watering the garden and the kids at the same time. It was another bright hot day, and Amanda stood on the front steps and looked around with her eyes squinched up, as if she were just coming out of the dark. When she saw David, she came over to him, skirting around the lawn and the splashing squealing kids.

"Come on," she said, "I want to talk to you."

"Go ahead," David said, "talk."

"Not here."

"Well, okay. In a minute. I can't quit now. I told them I'd hold the sprinkler for them, and they've just gotten started."

"Let them hold it themselves."

David shook his head. "Huh-uh," he said. "Dad said not to let them anymore. The last time they washed out two rose bushes and nearly drowned Esther."

Amanda sighed and started off disgustedly, but after a few steps she came back.

"Well, all right. We'll talk here, if we can hear each other. I wanted to tell you about the seance. It has to be tonight."

"Why tonight? I thought we were going to wait until Thursday night when Molly goes to her meeting."

"It has to be tonight," Amanda said. "I've been studying up, consulting the signs and omens. The signs are for tonight. We'll have to have it late, after Molly goes to bed."

"After Molly goes to bed? Wow! She never goes to bed until ten or eleven. Blair and Esther have never stayed up that late. They'd conk out for sure."

"Well, put them to bed at the regular time and then get them up again about midnight. That's the best time for a seance anyway."

David argued a little more, and even suggested that the seance be held without the kids, or at least without Blair and Esther; but Amanda wouldn't agree. She argued that a seance needed at least five people, in order to make their fingers touch when their hands were spread out on the table in front of them.

So David agreed doubtfully, and Amanda disappeared back into the house. David went on sprinkling the kids, and as he sprinkled, he worried a little about the seance; but at least he had one thing to be glad about. He was glad he hadn't gotten around to telling the kids about the poltergeist. If he had to get them up and take them to a seance in the middle of the night, he was just as glad they hadn't found out the house was haunted, or had been once. Finding out about a seance and a poltergeist all at once was enough to make anyone a little nervous, even a person a lot older than the kids were.

David had explained seances to the kids before; but when he told them about the one planned for that night, Esther had to know all over again just exactly what a seance was.

"I told you all about it," David said. "It's where you all sit down around a table in a dark room, and one of the people at the table is the medium. The medium goes into a trance and summons a spirit. Then the spirit talks to you or makes signals like making the table leg thump once for 'yes' and twice for 'no.' Sometimes you can even see the spirit, but not always."

"Who's going to get to be the medium?" Janie asked.

"Amanda."

"Why does Amanda always get to be everything? Why can't I be? I'm a lot more medium than she is."

"What do you mean, you're a lot more medium?"

"You and Amanda are biggest and Blair and Tesser are little, so I'm the medium."

David groaned. "That's an entirely different thing. This kind of medium is a person who has a special talent for contacting spirits. Not very many people can do it."

"Can Amanda do it?"

"She thinks she can. She said she hasn't had a chance to try in a real seance. But she's seen other people do it, and she knows how. She says she's been practicing for a long time. So if you're going to make a fuss about getting to be the medium, Janie, I'm just not even going to wake you up to go."

Janie frowned fiercely, but she nodded. "Okay. But the very next time we have a seance, it's *my* turn."

That night after the kids were in bed, David got comfortable with an interesting book to wait for Molly to go to bed. He didn't dare go to sleep himself for fear he wouldn't wake up in time. He took off his shoes and put on his pajama tops, in case Molly came in to say goodnight, and then he got into bed and started to read. Across the room in the other bed, Blair, who was as good at sleeping as Esther was at eating, was already very sound asleep.

David's book was one he had borrowed from Amanda. It was called *Stories of the Supernatural*, and it was all about ghosts who came back to avenge a wrong or to tell their terrible story to somebody. The longer David read, the more real the people and places in the stories became, and the easier it was for him to picture just exactly what everything looked and sounded like. In between each story he got up and went to the door to listen, but he could still hear the television going or Molly moving around downstairs. He was just finishing a story about a dead man who came back to haunt his old home in the shape of a horrible red-eyed dog, when he heard Molly's footsteps coming upstairs.

He was almost sure it was Molly. At least he couldn't make out any clicking toenail sound like there was in the dog story. But even so, David sat straight up in bed for a long time before he could bring himself to tiptoe to the door and look out. When he finally did, he could see the crack of light under Molly's door, so the foot-steps had been hers all right.

David went back to bed, then, to wait for Molly to get to sleep; but he didn't read anymore, and he didn't have any trouble stay-ing awake, either. He sat right in the middle of his bed, listening and thinking about the things he'd read. His ears had a stretched feeling and his eyes felt dry and bulgy by the time he heard the creak of Amanda's door. A moment later he heard a soft tap on his own.

Amanda stuck her head in and nodded. She was wearing her ceremonial robes, or at least part of them. When David got to the door, he noticed that she had on everything except the black stock-ings and high-button shoes. Instead she was wearing a pair of old floppy slippers.

Amanda noticed him looking and said, "The shoes are too noisy. You and the kids wear slippers, too."

"Should we wear the rest of our ceremonial robes?" David asked.

"Your ceremonial robes!" Amanda said. "Forget it!" But then she added, "Only the medium has to wear anything special at a seance. The rest of you can come as you are."

Amanda shuffled softly back to her room, and David got Blair up and sat him on the side of the bed. David had tried once or twice before to awaken Blair during the night, and he knew it wasn't easy; but he felt sure he could do it if he tried hard enough. Blair tipped over a couple of times, but after David shook him fairly hard, his eyes opened wide and stayed that way. David left him there and scooted down the hall to the girls' room. Janie and Esther woke up quite easily; but by the time David had hurried them back down the hall, Blair had tipped over again and was sound asleep. Finally David had Janie hold one side of Blair up, while he held the other, and they started for Amanda's room.

The room was completely dark except for the light of one small candle. David could barely see that the card table, covered by a blanket, stood in the center of the room with five chairs arranged around.

"Shh!" Amanda said as she let them in. She closed the door behind them and started giving orders. "You sit there, David. Stay away from that crow, Tesser. Janie you—"

"Not Janie," Janie interrupted. "My name is Calla."

"No," Amanda said. "That's only when *you* are practicing magic. Tonight you're just part of a seance. You don't have to be supernatural to do that. Janie, you—" she stopped, staring at Blair. "What's the matter with him?"

Blair was standing up, with David and Janie supporting him, but his eyes had gone shut again. David shook him and blew in his face, and his eyes got wide and stary again.

"Nothing's wrong with him," David said. "He's just not awake yet."

Amanda sighed. "Well, put him in the armchair so he won't fall over," she said. "And let's get going before my mother wakes up and comes snooping around."

154

As soon as everyone was at the table, Amanda started the same strange music she had played during the initiation, only very softly this time. Then she moved the candle to the center of the table. It was a small black candle, and it made a strong smell and very little light. Amanda took her place across from David. She had everyone spread out his hands on the table so that his thumbs touched and his little fingers touched the person's next to him.

David had to help Blair get his fingers arranged, and as soon as they were in place in front of him, Blair started leaning forward. His eyes were still wide open but very blank looking, and every few minutes David had to reach over and straighten him back up.

"Now," Amanda said, "I want you all to concentrate on the candle. Stare at the candle and try to keep from thinking of anything at all. I will go into a trance and when I have contacted a spirit, it will let us know that it is here."

"Wait," David said. "Don't we get to ask to talk to special spirits? Don't we get to say who we want to talk to?"

"Well, you do at some seances. I mean some mediums do it that way. But since I'm just starting, I thought I'd better just take whoever I can get. After I've had more practice, we'll try calling up special people. Who'd you want to talk to, anyway?"

"Well," David said, but then he didn't say anything more. His mind was too busy with some things he'd never let himself think through before. He'd known in a way, without admitting it even to himself, whom he was hoping to talk to. And he'd also known, or should have, what Amanda would say about it. After all, she'd already said plenty about blabbing too much to living parents, and she probably wouldn't feel any differently about talking to one who was dead.

David started to shake his head and say, "forget it," when he saw it was too late. Amanda was staring at him with a knowing expression on her face.

"Ooh, I get it," she said, raising her eyebrows and twisting her lip. "I get it."

"*No you don't!*" David said. "Forget it! Just forget it!"

"Okay," Amanda said, looking surprised. "Okay. Cool off. If people get uptight, it ruins the whole atmosphere for the seance. You have to be very relaxed and concentrate on thinking of absolutely nothing while I go into my trance."

"I'm not uptight!" David hissed in an angry whisper. He reached over and shoved his hand under Blair's face, which was almost down to the table again, and pushed him roughly back to a sitting position. Blair looked blankly at David and then smiled his Christmas card smile. After a minute David smiled back. After all, Blair couldn't help being sleepy and he certainly couldn't help the way Amanda acted. David put his hand on top of Blair's head and turned his face towards the candle.

"Just look hard at the candle, Blair," he said, "and concentrate."

"Just concentrate," Janie said. "Like this. See, Blair, this is how you concentrate." Janie was sitting very straight, staring at the candle. Her big eyes were round as circles and a little bit crossed.

Esther leaned over to see what Janie was doing. Then she said, "Like this? Look at me, Janie. Is this right?"

156

Janie glanced at Esther. "No," she said. "Your eyes aren't big enough. Make your eyes very big, like this."

"Will you be still!" Amanda hissed. She took hold of her head on each side as if she were about to pull out two handfuls of braid. "Those kids," she said accusingly to David. "Those kids are driving me crazy!"

But David was still mad enough at her that he wasn't about to feel guilty about what the kids were doing. Instead, he had to struggle to hold back a smile. But to his surprise, Janie apologized.

"We're sorry. We'll be quiet," Janie said. It was obvious that Janie was very enthusiastic about the seance, because she hardly ever said she was sorry about anything.

Amanda got up and started the record over because they already wasted such a lot of it, and then she came back and began to go into her trance. She leaned back in her chair with her face turned upward and her eyes closed. After a while she began to breathe very hard.

David stared at the candle and listened to the shrill monotonous music—and waited. He didn't know what he was waiting for. He wasn't angry any longer, or scared as he'd been back in his room, or hopeful. He really wasn't expecting much of anything. And for a long time nothing happened. Esther had several squirming fits; Janie sneezed and took her hand out of the circle to scratch her nose; and David had to take his hand out twice to keep Blair from collapsing on the table. He was beginning to feel a little sleepy himself when suddenly the table was jarred by a loud thump.

David jumped. Janie and Esther were sitting very still and wide-eyed, and even Blair seemed to be awake. The rap had been sharp and hard as if someone had hit the wood of the table with something metal, like a small hammer. David looked at everybody's hands. He was sure that none of them had moved from the circle.

Amanda was still sitting very still with her face turned upwards and her eyes closed. David wondered if she could have made the noise with her feet, but then he remembered the soft bedroom slippers. He was still wondering, when the rap came again. Two raps this time, close together.

"Who is there?" Amanda said in a strange hollow voice.

Rap!

"Are you a spirit?" Amanda asked.

Rap! The sound came again.

"Does one rap mean 'yes' and two mean 'no'?"

Rap!

David had to swallow hard before he could ask, "Are you the spirit of someone we know?"

Rap! Rap!

Then Esther asked, "Are you going to hurt us?"

Rap! Rap!

"That means no," Janie said. "It's not going to hurt us, Tesser."

"Are you coming here because you want to tell us something?" David asked.

Rap!

"Have you been here, to this house before?" Amanda asked.

158

Rap!

David leaned forward suddenly, staring at the spot in the middle of the table where the noise seemed to be coming from. "Are you the ghost that was here before? The poltergeist?"

There was a long pause, and then a very loud, *Rap!*

David choked, as if a breath on its way out had suddenly gone back instead. It wasn't really serious choking, but enough to make him cough.

Over his own coughing, he could hear Janie asking frantically, "What's a poltergeist? What's a poltergeist, David? What's a poltergeist, Amanda?"

"What's a who?" Esther said. "What is it, David?"

David was still coughing, and Amanda was still in her trance, but even in her trance she was frowning. David finally managed to stop coughing long enough to say, "Shhh! Shut up!"

Janie and Esther shut up, but it was too late. The ghost apparently had been chased away. David asked several more questions, but there were no more rapping noises. Amanda was still in her trance, eyes shut and breathing very hard. Now and then she moved, squirming around in her chair.

From somewhere behind Amanda there was suddenly a faint clicking noise, and a dim light appeared. It seemed to be coming from inside the closet, shining dimly through the curtain and the long strands of beads that Amanda had hung in front of the closet door. In the center of the faint glow of light, a dark shape emerged. It was indistinct but definitely human shaped—a round head with two long glowing eyes above a neck and shoulders.

159

David blinked his eyes and shook his head, but the figure stayed just the same.

Janie gave a little wail, and Esther began to catch her breath the way she always did before she began to cry. Then everything started happening at once. David lifted Esther out of her chair and started to the door with her, with Janie running right behind him. He put them outside the door and started back for Blair when he noticed that the light in the closet had disappeared. There was only Amanda, still sitting in her chair with her hands on the table and her eyes closed. The only light in the room was, again, the tiny flame from the black candle; but that was enough to let David see that all four of the other chairs were empty. Blair was nowhere to be seen.

For one horrible second David actually had some crazy idea that whatever it was they had seen in the glow from the closet had carried Blair off; but then he noticed a movement on the floor beside Blair's chair. There he was, all right, on his hands and knees, with just the back end of him sticking out from under the blanket that covered the table.

David grabbed Blair by the seat of his pajamas and pulled him out. Until he saw Blair's face he thought that Blair had been hiding, ostrich style, from the thing in the closet; but then he changed his mind, because Blair didn't look the least bit frightened. So he'd probably slept through the whole thing and finally tipped all the way out of his chair. But the fall—or something—had awakened him, because David didn't have to hold him up while he walked him out to where Janie and Esther were still huddled

together in the hall. David sent all three of them to wait in his room. Then he went back in to Amanda.

She was still sitting just as he had left her. David looked uneasily at the closet door. He went around the table to a place where he could see Amanda and the door at the same time.

"Amanda," he said. "Wake up."

Amanda moaned and rocked her head back and forth.

"Amanda," David said again, more loudly.

Her eyes opened slowly, and she looked around blank-eyed, as if she didn't know where she was.

"Where am I?" she said. "What happened?"

"The seance," David said. "Don't you remember? Don't you remember the rapping?"

Amanda shook her head. She stared right at David, open-eyed and innocent looking.

"You talked to it," David said.

"That must have been my contact talking. I don't remember."

"It made knocking noises. And we—we saw it. At least we saw something. In the closet."

Amanda turned around and looked at the closet door. Then she turned back to David.

"Tell me about it," she said.

Chapter Fifteen

AFTER DAVID GOT THE KIDS BACK IN BED AND WARNED THEM AGAIN NOT to talk about the seance, especially to Molly, he went back to Amanda's room. Amanda wanted him to tell her everything about what had happened after she went into her trance. David told her everything he could remember.

For the first few minutes, David kept getting the feeling he was making a fool of himself. After all if you looked at it in a reasonable scientific way, the way his father would probably look at it, it seemed pretty likely that Amanda hadn't really been in a trance at all—and that she knew perfectly well what had happened. In fact, she'd probably planned and arranged the whole thing herself. David couldn't figure out how; but he did know, from experience, how tricky Amanda could be. However, Amanda did look extremely innocent when she asked about what had happened, and she seemed genuinely surprised and excited to hear that the spirit had rapped "yes" when David had asked it if it were the poltergeist.

David didn't know what to think. He didn't know what to *think*, but—as far as *feeling* was concerned, he couldn't help feeling that *something* supernatural had been present, right there in Amanda's room.

The next day, out under the oak tree in the back yard, he talked about it again with the little kids. Janie was still trying to get David to explain what a poltergeist was, when Amanda came out of the house onto the back porch. When she saw David and the kids, she started across the yard towards them. She came slowly and seemed to be limping a little on her right foot.

"What's wrong with your foot?" David asked when she got close enough.

"I stubbed my toe on the door," Amanda said.

"Amanda," Janie interrupted, "what's a poltergeist, and when was it here before?"

Amanda told her all about it: what a poltergeist was and how there had been a famous one at Westerly House.

"And it came back again last night?" Janie asked. "Is it going to haunt the house again?"

"Well," Amanda said, "I don't know. But David said it rapped yes when he asked if it were the same poltergeist."

"Will it throw rocks and break things, like Amanda said?" Esther asked David. "Molly won't let it."

"No," David said. "I don't think so."

"Molly won't let it!" Amanda snorted in her most sarcastic

voice. "If it wants to it will, and Molly won't be able to do a thing about it. Nobody can tell a poltergeist what it has to do."

Blair hadn't said anything. He was probably listening because he listened a lot more than most people thought he did, but he seemed to be busy playing with a bluebird feather that he'd found under the tree. After everybody else had said everything they could think of about the seance and what happened there, David asked Blair a question.

"Did you hear the ghost rapping, Blair?"

Blair looked up from trying to push the feather through a buttonhole on his shirt. "Ghost rapping?" he asked. "No. I heard it talking."

"What are you talking about?" Amanda said. "Everybody else heard it rapping."

"You must have been having a dream," David said. "You were asleep most of the time."

"What did it say, Blair?" Janie asked. "What did it say to you?"

"It said it wasn't rapping. It said—" Blair stopped and looked up at Amanda and then at David. "It said—about Amanda."

"What's he talking about?" Amanda said. "He's making that up."

"What did it say about Amanda?" Janie asked.

"Shut up!" Amanda yelled at Janie. "He's making that up."

Everyone was looking at Blair. He leaned over and held out the blue feather to Amanda. "You can have my feather," he said. Then he wouldn't say anything else for a long time.

It wasn't long after lunch, that same day, that the rocks

started. David was in the kitchen with Molly, and Blair was there, too. David was talking to Molly when Esther came in from the hall limping and whimpering.

"What's the matter, Esther?" Molly asked.

"I stepped on a rock," Esther said.

She sat down on the floor and held up her foot, and there was a little red spot on the heel. Molly kissed it to make it well and told Esther that the skin wasn't broken and it would quit hurting in a minute.

"You must have stepped on it pretty hard," she said.

"I ran on it," Esther said. "In the hall."

"In the hall," David said. "What's a rock doing—" He stopped right in the middle of the sentence and went down the hall looking at the floor. Near the foot of the stairs he found a roundish pebble with one sharp edge. He picked it up and went on walking. In the living room he found another about the same size lying near the piano, and there were two more in the dining room. He took them back into the kitchen.

"Look," he said. "I found all these in the house. Did you bring them in, Blair?"

Blair shook his head, and Esther said she hadn't either. Molly took the rocks and looked at them thoughtfully.

"That's strange," she said. "I found some pebbles just outside my bedroom door this morning. Somebody must be playing with rocks."

David didn't say anything, but he suddenly had a crawling feeling on the back of his neck. He went looking for Janie to ask her if she'd been bringing rocks into the house, but he knew before he asked that she was going to say no.

Amanda was in her room again, but David knocked on the door and told her he had to talk to her.

When she saw the rocks, she looked excited but she only said, "The kids could have brought them in."

"No," David said. "I asked them, and they said they didn't."

"They could have been lying."

"Huh-uh. Esther doesn't lie, and Janie wouldn't lie about this. Janie only lies when she's telling a story."

"How about Blair? He wouldn't know whether he was lying or not."

That made David a little mad. "He would too," he said. "Blair knows a lot. He just knows different things from most people."

Amanda snorted. "Okay," she said. "Have it your way. Who do you think put them there?"

David only looked at her—significantly.

"The poltergeist?" Amanda asked.

"I—I thought about it," David admitted.

Amanda shrugged. "Well, if it was, we'll know soon enough."

"Why? How do you know that?"

"I mean—if it was the poltergeist, it will probably do something else pretty soon. It wouldn't just put a few rocks in the house and then stop."

David hadn't thought of it just that way, but he did after that. When the rock came flying into the kitchen that evening after dinner, it was almost as if he were expecting it.

The little kids had gone to bed; Amanda was in her room; and David was at the kitchen table looking through a big art book of Molly's. Amanda had washed the dishes before she went upstairs, but Molly was wiping off the counters and scrubbing the sink. Everything was very quiet when the rock flew into the room, bounced under the table and rolled out the other side. David looked out into the hall, but he almost knew there wouldn't be anyone there. Molly didn't know it, though. She picked up the rock, went to the kitchen door and looked up and down the hall.

"That's strange," she said. "Where do you suppose this came from?"

David only shook his head because he'd promised he wouldn't say anything to Molly. He had a feeling that she was going to find out anyway, before too long. But he wasn't going to be the one to tell her.

He was right about Molly finding out. The rocks kept coming. One came rattling down the hall and ended up against the front door, and at least three more came in through the kitchen door. Three at once clattered across the dining room, and Molly showed David a handful that had come through an open window of the sunroom that she used for a studio. David saw some of the rocks fall, or fly, and the kids saw some, and Molly saw several. In fact, one of the rocks that came in her studio window hit her on the arm.

On the second day after the rocks started, Amanda showed David a large pebble that she said had fallen in her room, while she was sitting right there, on her bed. She said it had been almost as

168

if the rock had fallen straight down from the ceiling. But except for that one rock, David didn't know of any that were thrown when Amanda was around. He wondered about that.

It was on the third or fourth day of the rock trouble that Molly called everyone into the living room for a serious talk. Of course she'd questioned all the kids before, but this time it was almost as if she were begging them to *please* tell her if they knew anything about the rocks. As soon as Molly started asking, all three of the little kids looked at David, and he knew they were asking if they could say anything about the poltergeist. David looked at Amanda.

Molly gave a nervous little laugh and said. "If it's not one of you kids playing some sort of a game, I'm almost beginning to think we're being haunted by one of those ghosts that throw things and make noises. What are they called?"

Molly was looking at Amanda, but Janie answered. "Poltergeists," she said. "They're called poltergeists."

"That's it," Molly said. "How did you happen to know about poltergeists, Janie?"

"Oh, I know an awful lot for my age," Janie said.

Molly laughed; but then she said that whether it was poltergeists or people playing games, it was beginning to make her very nervous and if it didn't stop pretty soon she was going to ask Mr. Ballard, the real estate man, to come over and take a look around.

That worried David. As soon as he had a chance, he talked to Amanda about it.

"We've got to keep her from talking to Mr. Ballard," he said.

"Why?" Amanda said.

169

"Because, he's almost sure to know about the Westerly poltergeist."

"So what?" Amanda said.

David stared at her. "You said not to let her know about the house being haunted. You were the one who said we absolutely weren't to tell her."

"I *said*," Amanda said, "that we shouldn't tell her. We can't help what Mr. Ballard does."

"But you said she'd be scared to death if she found out."

Amanda shrugged. "So what?" she said.

That night David thought for a long time about the way Amanda had said, "So what?" It was beginning to seem as if she really wanted Molly to find out that the house was haunted. All Amanda didn't want was for Molly to find out that the kids already knew about it. After he thought about it, David could believe that that was what Amanda really wanted, and that made him almost ready to believe worse things of Amanda. Except that he couldn't figure out how she was doing it.

He started looking for Amanda right after a rock fell. One time he found her in her room; another time she was walking toward the house from the garage, and when he asked, she said she'd been in the loft reading for a long time. But David went on having suspicions about Amanda and the rocks, until the day the milk pitcher got smashed.

They were all sitting around the dinner table at the time, Amanda and the four Stanley kids and Molly. During the whole meal everyone had seemed a little nervous and jumpy. David was thinking about the rocks, and he guessed everyone else was too, because they all seemed quiet and alert, like a bunch of birds keeping watch for danger even while they were eating.

Then, as if to make everything more nerve-wracking, the plumbing started having one of its noisy spells. The plumbing at the Westerly house was as old as everything else, and it kept having spells of what Molly called indigestion. The spells started with gurgles and went on to strange thumps and burping noises coming from different places in the pipes, especially from the water heater in the corner of the kitchen.

That evening the water heater had just given a particularly long loud gurgle that made everyone laugh, when there was a crash right in the middle of the table. David turned back from looking at the water heater in time to see a rock still rolling on the table and the milk still spreading from the broken milk pitcher.

Molly gasped and jumped up to go for the sponge and mop, and everyone else just sat there staring at the rock. Molly mopped up the milk looking frightened and angry at the same time.

"This has got to stop!" she said in a shaky voice. David wondered if she were talking to the family—or to the poltergeist. Nobody else said anything at all, not even Janie.

David thought about that while he was putting the kids to bed that night—how they all seemed to be doing less and less talking. He guessed he knew why, but he didn't like to think about it.

Thinking about it gave him a crawly feeling on the back of his neck. There was something uncomfortable in having to wonder who else was in earshot when you were talking to people in your own house. David knew that that was what everyone was wondering because it was what he was wondering himself, now that a rock had fallen when Amanda was right there before his eyes.

Chapter Sixteen

THAT SAME NIGHT, THE NIGHT THE ROCK SMASHED THE MILK PITCHER ON the kitchen table, everyone in the house was awakened in the middle of the night by a terrible crashing clatter. The noise went on crashing and thudding for what seemed like a very long time. David had time to sit straight up in bed, then duck back down under the covers, then start to peek back out again and reach for the light switch, before the last thud died away into silence.

The moment David finally found the light switch, he knew he hadn't imagined how long and loud the noise had been, because it had even awakened Blair.

Blair was sitting up in bed, and when the light went on he rubbed his eyes sleepily and said, "Noise. Was that a noise, David?"

"I'll say that was," David said. He put one leg out of bed and was just about to go look out the door, when the door flew open and Molly shot into the room. Her bathrobe was halfway on, her hair was every which-way, and her feet were bare.

"Are you all right?" she asked, and then she turned and ran out of the room before David had time to answer. David got to the door in time to see her running into Janie and Esther's room. The door of Amanda's room was open, and the light was on, so Molly had probably already checked to see if Amanda was all right. A couple of minutes later Molly came back down the hall with Janie and Esther running behind her. When she saw David in the door to his room, with Blair peeking out from behind him, she stopped and tried to smile.

"Well," she said. "What do you suppose that was, an earthquake?"

"I don't think so," David said. "I didn't feel anything shake, anyway. But I sure heard it."

"I heard it, too," Janie said.

"Me too," Esther said. "I heard it, too. Did you hear it, Blair?"

Janie grabbed David's arm and whispered loudly towards his ear, "It was the poltergeist, wasn't it, David? Wasn't it the poltergeist?"

"Shut up, Janie," David whispered back. In a louder voice he said, "It sounded to me as if it came from the stairs."

"I know," Molly nodded. "I think so, too." She put her arms around Janie and Esther and hugged them up against her. Then she turned slowly towards the end of the hall where the stairs began. Watching her, David saw that her face was puckered around the eyes. "The sound must have come from the stairs," she said.

Just then Amanda came out of her room. She had on the old

shirt of her father's that she always used for a nightgown, and her eyes were squinty as if she were still half asleep.

"What was it?" she asked.

Everyone shook his head.

"It seemed to come from the stairs," Molly said, and started walking in that direction again with all the kids right behind her.

When Molly switched on the light at the top of the stairs, everyone gasped. Starting almost at the top, all the way down to the landing, and on down to the downstairs hall, the stairs were covered with dirt, broken chunks of pottery and occasional shredded pieces of split-leaf philodendron.

"Ohhh!" Molly said. "My poor plant."

Molly had had the split-leaf philodendron for a long time. It had outgrown its planter a long time before when Dad and Molly were still just going together, and Dad had brought home the huge pottery planter from a field trip to Mexico. By the time Dad and Molly had gotten married, the plant had grown to be almost as tall as Dad. When they moved into the Westerly house, the only empty spot Molly could find that was big enough for it was in the bay window at the end of the upstairs hall, near the top of the stairway. David had helped Dad carry the heavy planter up the stairs, and all the way up Dad had grumbled in a joking way about "why couldn't Molly have found a good place for such a heavy thing at the bottom of the stairs." It was at the bottom of the stairs now, all right. At least most of the main stem was, along with a scatter of dirt and a couple of big chunks of the pottery planter.

"How—" Molly began. "How on earth—" Her hands were in a shaky cup around the bottom of her face, but David could see her eyes, and they looked as if she might be going to cry.

Esther pushed past David and started down the stairs, picking up pieces of pottery and broken leaves. Everyone else just stood there silently watching her. They watched her stop, when her hands were full, and come back up the stairs, carefully putting one foot and then the other on each stair. At the top of the stairs she made a neat little pile of the pieces and started down for more.

Then Molly finally took her hands away from her mouth and said, "Tesser darling, not now. We'll clean it up in the morning. Let's all just forget it for now and go back to bed."

Molly held out her hand to Esther, and Esther took it, but she looked back over her shoulder uneasily at the mess on the stairs. Messes always worried Esther, no matter who made them.

As David started back to his room, he heard Molly asking Amanda if she'd like to spend the rest of the night with her, instead of alone in her own room. David left the door open and listened to hear what Amanda said. He couldn't hear all of it, but he got enough to know that Amanda said she didn't want to, and that not everybody was terrified by anything the least bit supernatural.

Then he heard Janie say, "We'll stay with you, Molly. May Tesser and I stay in your room with you tonight? We want to, don't we, Tesser?" So David closed the door and went to bed.

David stayed awake for a long time listening and waiting, but nothing else happened, and finally he went to sleep. When he woke up the next morning, Molly was already up and she must have been up for some time, because the remains of the philoden-dron were entirely gone.

Everything was very strange and tense at breakfast that morn-ing. Of course, everyone was thinking about the poltergeist and the plant, and at first the kids started to talk about it, but Molly begged them not to. Her face looked pale and tired, and she seemed very nervous and jumpy. After the little kids had finished and gone out-side to play, David asked her if she had called Mr. Ballard.

Molly nodded. "Yes," she said. "I did. But he wasn't exactly helpful. He told me he had heard that at one time, years ago, there were rumors about Westerly House being haunted. But that was very long ago, and there has been absolutely no trouble for years or he wouldn't have accepted the responsibility of finding a buyer for the house. He made it clear that he isn't a superstitious person, himself, and that he thinks I am just imagining things because I'm nervous about my husband being away."

"Huh!" David said. "I guess he'd say we all just imagined about what happened last night."

"I tried to tell him about it," Molly said. "But he just said that probably one of the children had done it and was afraid to confess."

"Well, if he means the little kids, he's crazy," David said. "For one thing they couldn't. It was too heavy. And for another, if any one of them had done it, I'd know it."

"I know," Molly said. "I don't think you children did it. Not any of you."

As she said that, Molly's chin started wiggling as if she were

177

going to cry, and she turned away so David and Amanda couldn't see her face and hurried out of the room.

David looked at Amanda. "What do you think?" he asked. "About her, I mean? Is she going to crack up, or something."

Amanda shrugged. "I don't see what she's so scared about. Poltergeists don't ever really hurt anyone. At least not that I've ever heard of. Oh, I read about one that stuck people with pins and pinched them, but nothing really serious. There was one I read about that haunted a house in England for about three years that—" And Amanda started to tell a long story about a particular poltergeist and what it did. But David didn't listen too carefully because he was thinking about the thing she'd said about three years. He was wondering how anyone could stand a poltergeist for that long. He was pretty sure he couldn't, and the way things were going he didn't see how Molly was going to stand it even for the nine more days before Dad was due to come home.

Except for a few pebbles that Janie found scattered around the dining room, nothing happened during that day. Amanda spent most of the day in her room, as usual, and the kids played outdoors on the lawn and under the oak tree. Molly didn't do much painting. Instead she gardened some and sat in the lawn chair holding a book but not reading it much. Dinner came and went without any trouble.

After dinner Molly let the little kids stay up later than usual, and about ten o'clock everyone went to bed at once. Esther and Janie spent the night again in Molly's room.

Blair went to sleep right away as usual, but David was beginning to think he was never going to go to sleep when he suddenly found himself waking up with the feeling that he'd been asleep for a long time. He also had the feeling that he'd been awakened by something in particular, but just for a second he didn't know what it had been. He lay perfectly still trying to reach back into his sleep and remember what had awakened him—and then it came back. Something had touched his shoulder.

The instant David's mind said "something touched me" his heart went THUD and his eyes jerked towards his right shoulder—and a solid wall of darkness. He lay perfectly still under the blankets, stiff as a statue and just as motionless, except for his heart, which was beating so loudly that whatever it was, standing there in the darkness beside him, could surely hear it too.

Then it touched him again, and at the same instant a soft familiar voice said, "David."

David had to gulp hard before he could answer. "Blair. What are you doing out of bed?"

"David," Blair said. "I'm listening. Are you listening?"

"What are you talking about?" David said. "Get back to—"

But Blair shook David's shoulder again and said, "Shhh!"

David hushed for a second, and in that second he heard it, too. It was a soft squeaking sound, and it came from another part of the house. David sat up in bed and reached for Blair in the darkness. Blair felt familiar—very small and warm. They sat on the edge of the bed together and listened.

After a minute they heard the noise again—a soft distant squeak, followed this time by a very soft click. David stood up, and

179

still holding on to Blair, he felt his way toward the bedroom door. David's groping hand had just found the doorknob when somewhere downstairs there was a loud crash, and then almost immediately, another even louder one.

David jerked the door open and peered out into the darkness. At the same instant a light appeared at the bottom of the stairs and came bounding up them. Bounding, as if carried by someone who was running, skipping three or four stairs at a time. The beam was small and narrow, but as it reached the top of the stairs, it was enough to let David see that the person carrying the light was small and dressed in white. The light skimmed noiselessly down the hall and disappeared into Amanda's room.

The light came on, then, in Molly's room, and Molly came running out into the hall, halfway into her bathrobe again, the way she'd been the night before. When she had disappeared into Amanda's room, David turned on his own light and he and Blair started down the hall. They met Molly outside Amanda's room.

"Oh, David," Molly said. "What are we going to do?"

"Where's Amanda?" David asked.

"In bed," Molly said. "She's all right. But that awful, awful noise—"

Molly was terribly frightened. Frightened enough to quit trying to pretend that she wasn't in front of David and the kids. David suddenly felt angry. He was on the verge of saying something very drastic, when Amanda came out of her room and Janie and Esther came running out of Molly's, all at the same time. Amanda was blinking her eyes again and looking very sleepy.

"I—I suppose I'd better go see what it was this time," Molly said.

"Me too," Janie said. "We'll all go. Won't we, David?"

"Sure," David said. "We'll all go." But when everyone started down the stairs, he waited. He waited until they turned the corner at the bottom of the stairs, and then he dashed into Amanda's room. By her bed, on her nightstand, was the little pen-sized flashlight that David had noticed there before. David picked it up for a second, then put it back where it had been and ran out and down the stairs.

He reached the living room almost as soon as everyone else did, just as they were discovering what had made the noise. A painting had fallen off the wall.

It was a large oil painting that Molly had done of Janie and the twins. They found it lying on the floor beneath the spot where it had been hanging, but it hadn't just fallen by itself. They knew it hadn't as soon as they saw the place near the top where the heavy gilt frame was badly smashed. Near the painting, on the floor, they found the heavy round hunk of rock crystal that Dad kept on his desk to use as a paperweight. The crystal was heavy—and it must have been thrown very hard.

David kept his mouth tightly closed while he helped Molly pick things up and get the kids back to bed. He kept it closed because he had a feeling that if he started talking he'd say a lot. And before he did that, he wanted a chance to think. He wanted a chance to think some more about Amanda's flashlight, which had still been warm when he picked it up.

Chapter Seventeen

WHEN DAVID FINALLY GOT BACK INTO BED THAT NIGHT, HE FULLY INTENDED
to stay awake until he had everything thought out. There was a lot
to think over—like *why?* and *how?* and maybe most important,
what now? But to his surprise, he almost immediately went to sleep.

That is, he woke up the next morning, surprised to find that
he had gone to sleep before he'd decided anything at all. He knew
he'd have to get up soon, so he skipped over the *why?* and *how?*
and concentrated on *what now?* What was he, David, going to do
about the fact that Amanda had been the poltergeist all along?

The first thing he wondered about was what would happen
when everybody knew. What would Molly do, and, most of all,
what would Dad do? When Dad found out about everything that
had happened, and how frightened everyone had been, what
would he do? The Westerly girls had been sent away to boarding
school, and no one had even proved that they had anything to do

with their poltergeist. Where would they send Amanda? And after she'd been punished and sent away, how would she feel about adults—when she already hated nearly all of them?

That was about as far as David's thinking had taken him when Blair woke up and came over to sit on David's bed. It suddenly occurred to David that Blair would have to be a part of whatever he decided because Blair had been right beside him when Amanda ran up the stairs.

"Did you see someone run up the stairs last night?" David asked, just to find out how much Blair knew.

Blair nodded. "Amanda," he said.

"Are you going to tell on her?" David asked.

Blair ran his finger around on the bed following the star shaped pattern of the quilt, but David knew he'd heard and was thinking about it. Finally he smiled at David and shook his head no.

"We could tell her we know," David said, "but that we weren't going to tell anyone else if she stops doing things. She'd probably stop if we did that, but she'd sure be mad at us. And she'd probably keep thinking we were going to tell any day—for years and years. It wouldn't make her very easy to live with."

Blair nodded.

"The best way would be to make her stop without telling anybody anything. I've been thinking about how to do it."

"Make her stop," Blair said. He crawled under the bedspread and then sat up, making a small tepee shape in the middle of the bed. He sat very still under the spread for a long time.

Finally David asked, "What are you doing under there?"

184

"I'm thinking," Blair said. "I'm making Amanda stop."

David laughed and kicked him, and Blair tipped over and crawled out with his curly hair all smashed down on his forehead.

Molly came in then and told them it was time to get up, so there wasn't time to come to a decision, at least not right then. But when Amanda came down to breakfast, late as usual, David felt different about her. He watched her look around at everyone, particularly at her mother, as if she were trying to see how much they had been upset by the picture falling the night before. When she looked at David, he did something he hadn't planned to do—he stared back at her. It was a long straight look—the kind of cool look he'd never been able to get just right before. But what surprised him was it wasn't really cool at all, because what was really behind it was anger.

When Molly joined the rest of them at the table, she said that she'd just called up an old friend who was going to come and stay with them for a few days.

"Who?" Amanda asked. "Not Ingrid, I hope."

"Yes, Ingrid," Molly said. "I know you don't like her, but she'll be free for the next three days, and she says she'll stay even longer and commute to work if I need her. I just think I'll feel a lot better if there's another adult in the house with us."

When Molly started talking to Janie, David asked Amanda, "Who's Ingrid?"

"Just a friend of my mother's. They used to work together. I don't like her."

"Why not?"

Amanda shrugged. "She's a typical adult, nosey and bossy."

After breakfast, when Amanda headed for the loft to read, David went with her. He didn't know why for sure, except that keeping his eyes on her as much as possible might keep her from pulling any more poltergeist tricks. Might, and might not. David hadn't forgotten how the rock had fallen on the kitchen table when Amanda was right there in front of them, or the mysterious things that happened during the seance, while Amanda's hands were out on the table the whole time.

In the loft, Amanda asked David if he and the kids were going to ride into the city with Molly when she went to get Ingrid.

"I don't think so," David said. "The kids don't like drives much, and besides there wouldn't be room for all of us and Ingrid."

"It'll take her at least two hours," Amanda said. "Aren't you and the kids going to be scared to stay here alone all the time?"

"Aren't you?" David asked. He was wondering what kind of poltergeist trick Amanda was planning to get set up while everybody was gone.

"Me?" she said. "I might be a little nervous, but if you're used to supernatural manifestations, you don't worry too much about things like pictures falling off the wall. But the kids will be scared to stay alone, won't they?"

David shrugged. "The twins won't mind. They're old enough to know that ghosts and things like that are supposed to be scary, but they're not really old enough to understand why. They won't be scared unless somebody else is."

"How about Janie?"

"Oh, she's scared. But she kind of enjoys being scared. The best day Janie ever had was once when she almost got run over by a car. She must have told everybody all about it a thousand times."

"And how about you?" Amanda asked. "You don't seem very scared." She was watching David closely through narrowed eyes.

Just a minute before David had been thinking, again, about telling Amanda what he and Blair had seen; but because she seemed about to guess, it was suddenly important not to let her know.

"I guess I'm getting used to supernatural manifestations, too," he said. He collapsed in the dusty hay and pretended to be sleepy, but he kept his eyes open enough so that he could watch Amanda from under his eyelashes. She went back to her book, but every now and then she stopped and looked at David strangely, as if she couldn't quite figure something out.

Molly didn't leave for the city until the middle of the afternoon because Ingrid couldn't be picked up until she was through working. Before she left, Molly talked to David and Amanda for a long time about what they should do. They should all stay together as much as possible, and if anything did happen, they were to try not to frighten Janie and the twins. She told Amanda to put some potatoes on to bake about 5:30, and she and Ingrid would be home in time to make the rest of the dinner.

Molly looked very tense and worried. As she got into her little car, she tried to smile cheerfully at Amanda and David, but it wasn't a very successful attempt.

"It'll be all right," David said. "I don't think we're going to have any poltergeist trouble today. I just have a feeling." He didn't go on and explain that Amanda probably wouldn't bother to poltergeist when there were only kids around to scare.

After Molly left, Amanda went to her room and shut herself in, so David took the kids to his room and read them a story. But he was careful to leave his door open and sit where he could see the door to Amanda's room. Janie was sitting on the arm of the chair, where she always sat so she could read along, Esther was sitting on the floor in front of him, and Blair sat on David's bed. At least he sat there for a while, and then he curled up there and before long he was sound asleep.

David's tongue was beginning to get tired when Amanda came out of her room and came in to see what they were doing. She listened to David read for a while, and then she offered to take a turn. Janie frowned.

"David reads better than anybody," she said.

Amanda gave her an icy look. "Last year," she said, "I was reading four years above grade level."

"David reads five years above," Janie said.

"No I don't, Janie," David said. "They just like the way I read," he told Amanda, "with lots of expression. Our Mom used to read to us a lot, and she read with lots of expression, so I learned how."

"Not even the library lady reads as good as David," Esther said.

"When David reads," Janie said, "he makes his voice like the music on television. It gets scary in the scary parts, and it tells you when something is about to happen."

Amanda snatched the book away from David and began to read. She read with a *great* deal of expression. After a while Janie and Esther started looking pleased and settled down to listen. Blair went on sleeping on David's bed.

Two or three times Janie or Esther interrupted to say that Amanda was a very good reader, and then Amanda went on reading with more expression than ever. Actually, David thought she was overdoing it a bit, but he didn't say so because it occurred to him that there were worse things she might be overdoing if she weren't busy reading. But finally he did remind her that it was 5:30 and time to put the potatoes on to bake. Amanda finished the chapter, and they all went down to the kitchen. All except Blair who was still asleep.

It was a little bit past six when the phone rang. It was Molly. She was calling from a service station about halfway between the city and Steven's Corners. She sounded a little bit frantic. Something had happened to her car, and she and Ingrid were waiting for it to be fixed.

"Is everything all right there?" she kept asking.

"Sure," David said. "Everything is just fine. Nothing has happened at all. Not even any rocks."

"That's wonderful, David," Molly said. "Maybe you and Amanda had better fix dinner for yourselves and the kids. We have to have a new water pump for the car, and they didn't have one the right size. One of the mechanics has gone for one, and he should be back soon. But we may not be home for another hour or so. Will that be all right?"

Amanda was fairly cheerful about having to cook for the kids. While she and David fried the hamburgers and put the peas on to

189

cook, she kept mentioning how much Janie and Esther had liked her reading.

When dinner was almost ready, Blair came downstairs looking very sleepy and climbed up into his chair. Dinner was quite unusual that night, partly because the hamburger was a little burnt and the peas were raw, but also because of the way Amanda acted when there were no adults there. She talked and laughed and fought with Janie in a friendly way about whether raw vegetables were better for you than cooked ones. After dinner she offered to help get the kids ready for bed.

It was a little earlier than their regular bedtime, but Janie and Esther said they wanted to go to bed. Maybe because they were enjoying the novelty of having Amanda pay so much attention to them. Blair said he wasn't sleepy.

"No wonder," David said. "You slept most of the afternoon."

Blair watched Amanda riding Esther up the stairs on her back and decided that he'd go to bed, too. When Amanda came back for him, he climbed on her back.

"I thought you weren't sleepy?" David said.

"Maybe I am," Blair said. "Sometimes I don't know."

The phone rang again while Amanda was still helping Esther take her bath, and David answered it. It was Molly again, and she was still at the service station. The mechanic who had gone after the part for the car had to go to three places before he found one the right size. He'd just gotten back with it, and it would take at least another hour before Molly and Ingrid could get home. Molly asked three times if everything was all right.

"Everything's great," David said. "We finished dinner, and we're putting the kids to bed. There hasn't been any sign of the poltergeist. I think it may have moved out."

Molly laughed a little and said she certainly hoped so and hung up. David went into the parlor and turned on the TV. He sat there staring at it but not really seeing it. He was really thinking about what he had said and wondering if he really believed it. Had Amanda stopped being a poltergeist, or had she only stopped temporarily, because she really wasn't interested in scaring kids? David was still wondering when Amanda came back downstairs and sat down at the other end of the couch.

"Wow," she said. "Those kids are a lot of work. How do you stand it?" But she didn't sound as if she really thought it was all that bad.

They'd been sitting there, watching the TV, for about half an hour when Amanda got up and started for the kitchen. She called back to David that she was going for some cookies and did he want some. David said yes, and went back to watching the tube, because he was very interested in a murder that was about to happen. Amanda hadn't been gone more than a minute when there was a very quiet moment on the TV—while the murderer was climbing silently in a window—and in the middle of the silence, David heard a small but definite noise that seemed to come from the hallway or stairs. He turned off the TV and was standing there listening when something, a whole avalanche of things, started bouncing down the stairs. There were big bumps and thumps like something very heavy, and smaller thumps, and a clattering rumble like hundreds of bouncing rocks. David was still listening to the last of the clatter when from the direction of the kitchen there came a high-pitched scream.

David started for the stairs, turned and started for the kitchen, and then turned back again towards the stairs. While he was running in circles, he was thinking parts of things like, "What did she do?" and "Why did she do it?" and "What did she throw down the stairs?" and then, "If she threw it, who just screamed in the kitchen?"

When he finally made it to the foot of the stairs, he found himself in the midst of a floor full of rocks—pebbles mostly, but some larger ones. As he bent to pick one up, David heard a sound behind him and whirled to find Amanda standing a foot or two away. Her hands were clasped in front of her mouth, and her eyes looked like owl eyes, round and unblinking. David stared at her, but this time she didn't stare back. Instead she leaned to peer around him up the stairs.

"What's that?" she asked in a thin unnatural voice.

David looked where she was pointing. The object was balanced on the edge of a stair, fairly near the bottom of the flight. David climbed, picking his way among rocks, and picked it up. When he turned to show it to Amanda, she was so close behind him that he nearly hit her with it.

"What is it?" Amanda asked again.

"I was about to ask you," David said pointedly. But Amanda didn't seem to get the point.

"I—I don't know," she said, staring at the thing in David's hands.

192

Watching her, David couldn't help being impressed with her acting ability. She really did look and act frightened. Turning his attention to the object in his hands, David decided that it must be the insides of some kind of clock or mechanical toy. Whatever it was, it was very old and rusty and covered with dust.

"There's something else," Amanda whispered.

A few steps farther up David picked up what seemed to be a very large slingshot. Like the wind-up machinery, it had a dusty feel to it, and the wide strip of elastic that hung from one of the prongs was limp and rotten. Holding the dusty slingshot, David felt a strange prickling sensation at the back of his neck, and he turned and peered on up the stairs. The upstairs hall light was off so it was very shadowy on the landing, but he could see something else sitting there, something large and dark.

The object on the landing turned out to be a box. A wooden box, long and narrow, and strongly made. As David reached the landing with Amanda right beside him, he could see that the box was on its side and scattered around it were many more rocks and pebbles. Most of the rocks were very small, but there seemed to be one that was much larger.

The larger object was roughly round, and in the dim light David was sure it was only a larger rock—until he had it in his hand. But then he saw that it wasn't a rock at all. It was a head, the carved and varnished head of a wooden cupid.

Chapter Eighteen

DAVID AND AMANDA BOTH STOOD STARING AT THE CUPID'S HEAD IN David's hands for several seconds before David put it down on the landing and wiped his hands. His hands were grainy with dust, and his neck and back were crawly with nervousness, even though he knew, or almost knew, that Amanda had done the whole thing—somehow.

He looked at Amanda, but she was busy looking all around her, turning and peering with quick jerky movements. She looked up and down the stairs, over the banisters into the hall below, and up along the edge of the stairwell over their heads. When her eyes finally came back to David, they had a puckered look at the corners, almost as if she were going to cry.

"What are we going to do, David?" she said in a voice that sounded almost like a wail.

David opened his mouth, but he was so puzzled that nothing came out. He knew that Amanda must have done it—but he really didn't see how she could have. How could she have gotten back into the kitchen in time to scream there, almost before the rocks had stopped bouncing down the stairs? He knew, though, how smart and tricky she was, and he could almost believe that she'd found a way. What was getting harder and harder to believe was that she could do such an absolutely great job of pretending to be scared half out of her wits.

Suddenly Amanda grabbed his arm and said, "Let's get out of here. Let's get back where it's lighter, in the living room."

When they got to the living room, Amanda decided the kitchen might be better, but then she decided on the living room again—and they wound up sitting on the couch. David sat at one end, and Amanda sat very close to him.

"David," Amanda said suddenly, "please tell me the truth. You didn't do it, did you? I guess you couldn't have really. You were right here in the living room, and I'd only been gone a minute when it happened. I guess you couldn't have. But did you, David? Please tell me if you did."

"No," David said. "I didn't do it. Did you?"

"No-o-o," Amanda said, wailing again. "I didn't do it. I didn't! Not this time."

"Not this time?"

Amanda looked startled for a minute, but then she nodded. "I did the rest of it. All the rest of it. But I didn't do what happened tonight. I didn't."

David had a strange feeling that Amanda was telling the truth. And along with it, he had an even stranger feeling that he'd known it all along. That crawly feeling on the back of his neck hadn't been for nothing.

"Wow!" David said softly.

"I'm scared," Amanda said. "I wish Mom and Ingrid would get here. David, aren't you scared?"

"Sure," David said. "I'm scared."

"You don't seem scared," Amanda said in a chattery voice. "Out there, on the stairs, you didn't seem scared at all."

It flashed in David's mind to say that he hadn't been scared then because he already knew that Amanda had done the rest of it and he was still halfway sure she'd done the new thing, too. But he didn't say it. He wasn't sure why he didn't, except that having Amanda think he was brave somehow made him feel braver. And he had a feeling that he might need all the bravery he could get before Molly got back.

For an eternity—that probably lasted not more than twenty minutes—David and Amanda huddled together on the couch and talked in whispers about all the stuff on the stairs, and the cupid's head, and the poltergeist.

The head had been missing since the time the poltergeist had taken it, years and years before. No one had seen it in all that time. And suddenly it was back. It had come back and with it had come hundreds of rocks, and some old junk and, weirdest of all, the dust. On the head itself, and in the box, and all over the landing there was dust. Not outdoorsy, earthy dust, but old moldy smelling dust, the kind you might find in ancient deserted places closed off from air and life.

But wherever it had come from, the head was back, and something had to have brought it. And it really looked as if that something was the poltergeist.

It was Amanda who brought up the question of why. If the poltergeist had come back to Westerly House, after all that time, *why* had it come? As soon as she asked, she stopped and stared at David, and David knew what she was thinking, because he was thinking the same thing. He was wondering if the poltergeist had come back because Amanda had been impersonating it. Perhaps it hadn't liked Amanda pretending to be it. It was a frightening thought, even to David, and Amanda looked positively sick with terror.

They stopped talking then and sat quietly watching and listening. The house was perfectly silent. After a while David began to relax a little, and he wanted to ask Amanda some questions about how she had done the other poltergeist things; but looking at her pale, tight face, he decided she wasn't in the mood to talk about it.

Amanda and David were still crouching quietly in the corner of the couch when they heard the sound of Molly's car in the driveway. Nothing in the world ever sounded so good.

"They're home," they said to each other, and made a dash for the garage. They were halfway through the story before Molly and Ingrid were clear out of the car. Of course they had to go back over it several times before the women began to understand what they were talking about. When they did, Molly put her arms around

Amanda and said, "Oh dear, I was so afraid something like this would happen."

The next thing Molly did was to rush upstairs with the rest of them right behind her to check on the little kids. All three of them were sleeping peacefully. On their way back down the stairs, Molly and Ingrid carefully inspected the mess on the stairs. When they were all back down in the living room, Ingrid started asking a million questions.

Ingrid was large and blond and perfectly logical. She even looked logical, as if she'd been planned with a slide rule. Her favorite expression was "it follows," and it was evident that if something didn't "follow" logically she didn't have a bit of respect for it. It was also obvious that a real ghost didn't logically follow any ideas or experiences that Ingrid had ever had. Ingrid suspected somebody human, like David or Amanda, or both.

Ingrid's suspicions had a strange effect on Amanda. As soon as Ingrid started asking suspicious questions, the color began to come back into Amanda's face and her lips quit shaking and began to curl downward in her upside-down smile. She clearly didn't intend to tell Ingrid anything, and David went along with it. If Amanda wanted to wait for another time to tell about the part she had played in the other poltergeist manifestations, it was all right with him. Besides, there was something about the way Ingrid obviously didn't believe a word you were saying when you were telling the truth that made you almost want to lie to her.

If Ingrid didn't believe anything David and Amanda said,

Molly seemed to be believing all of it. She sat next to Amanda on the couch, looking as jumpy and shaky as Amanda had before Ingrid got her mad.

When Ingrid finally decided to postpone the rest of the third degree until the next morning, David offered to help her clean up the mess on the stairs. So Amanda stayed in the living room with Molly while David and Ingrid picked up all the rocks and other things and put them in the wooden box. Back on the landing among the rocks and the moldy dust, David was almost glad for Ingrid's company. In a situation like that, you couldn't help appreciating a person who never had believed in ghosts and never would believe in ghosts, no matter what happened.

When all the rocks were in the box, David picked up the cupid's head and dusted it off.

"I want to keep this," he said.

When Ingrid asked him why, in the tone of voice a cop might use to ask a guy at the bank teller's window why he was wearing a mask, David just shrugged. "I just want to keep it in my room," he said.

"Where have you *been* keeping it?" she asked.

David shook his head at her, slowly. "I haven't," he said—but she didn't believe it. David could see that nothing he could say would make any difference, so he didn't try. Besides, he wasn't too sure himself why he wanted the cupid's head. Except that he had thought about putting it back where it came from. That headless cupid had always bothered him a little, and he liked the idea of giving it back its head after all those years without it.

Molly and Amanda were still sitting on the couch, talking, but they suddenly got quiet when David and Ingrid came back into the room. David was curious about what they'd been discussing because he sensed a difference. He couldn't put his finger on anything, but the difference was there all right, so strong David could almost feel it in the air around them.

Ingrid slept in Amanda's room that night, and Amanda spent the night in her mother's room. That was different, too. David was so curious that a while later, when he was on his way to the bathroom, he stopped for a minute outside the door of Molly's room. He wasn't really eavesdropping because he couldn't hear what they were saying, but he could hear them talking and talking, as if they were going to keep it up for half the night.

Back in his own room, David lay awake for a long time. He thought about Amanda and her mother still talking in the next room. Probably making more conversation in one night than they'd done in the last year or two. He also thought about the cupid's head, just a few feet away in the top drawer of his dresser. Then he thought about the things on the stairs and wondered again who had put them there—and came to the same conclusion as before. There just wasn't any logical way to explain it, no matter what Ingrid said.

But somehow, the idea didn't scare him very much. Maybe you could get used to the idea of living with a ghost, and once you were used to it, it didn't scare you anymore. David wondered if that were true.

As a test he pictured to himself the door of his room opening silently and then his underwear drawer sliding slowly out, pulled by an unseen hand, as the poltergeist returned to claim its head. David raised up on one elbow and pictured the whole thing very clearly. In the dim moonlight that flooded his room, it wasn't a difficult thing to do.

He decided it must be true, all right, about getting used to ghosts. No matter how realistically he pictured the poltergeist, nothing crawled at the back of his neck. In fact, after a while he grinned in the direction of the dresser drawer.

"Okay, poltergeist," he said out loud. "You had it first. It's on the right side, just behind the socks."

Chapter Nineteen

THE NEXT MORNING THE CUPID'S HEAD WAS STILL THERE, ON THE RIGHT HAND side, behind the socks. If it hadn't been there, David might have had a hard time believing that the whole thing had happened at all. For one thing, it was the kind of clear bright day that makes everything look very solid and sharply defined and unmysterious. The kind of day that makes you wonder how on earth you could even have imagined the weird stuff you believed in at midnight.

Another thing that made the night before hard to believe was Ingrid. Ingrid was up early that morning, taking charge of everything. It's not easy to take charge of what other people believe or don't believe, but if anyone could do it, Ingrid could. Watching Ingrid bustling around the house, David found himself definitely leaning toward a logical explanation for what had happened the night before. Not that he had one. He just found himself looking in directions where one might be.

Of course, the best direction was still Amanda. David found himself watching Amanda very closely. At breakfast she was very quiet as usual, but David still sensed a difference about her. At least he did until Ingrid started asking questions again and Amanda's guard went up as cool and hard as ever.

Ingrid asked a lot of questions. All the ones she asked the night before, and a lot of new ones. Some of the new ones were about Janie and the twins, who hadn't yet come downstairs to breakfast. Ingrid wanted to know how long the kids had been in bed before the stuff was thrown downstairs, and where they'd been when some of the other poltergeist things had happened.

When Molly saw what Ingrid was driving at, she shook her head. "They couldn't have had anything to do with it, Ingrid," she said. "They're too little. I don't think we ought to mention it to them at all. They've had too many upsetting events in their lives lately. I'm just glad they all slept through it last night."

Ingrid didn't agree but she finally promised not to mention it to the twins, at least, but she still thought she ought to question Janie. Molly and Ingrid were still arguing about Janie, when Amanda excused herself and went out the back door. After a minute David followed her. She was sitting on the back steps in the morning sun. David sat down beside her.

The sun was warm on the steps, but the air still had the night-freshened cool of summer mornings. Amanda and David sat there looking at the ground and not saying anything. The ground was dry and bare by the back steps, and not all that interesting, but the questions David had in mind weren't easy to get started on, so he studied the ground instead. Amanda seemed to be doing the same thing. David was beginning to think they might sit there all morning when an ant crawled by carrying a dead beetle about three times his size. David and Amanda both looked at the ant.

"Wow," they both said at once.

After they'd both said something about "how on earth did it carry something so much heavier than it was," David turned to Amanda and said, "How—" and before he could ask any more she answered.

"I kind of rolled it," she said. "You remember how the planter was kind of rounded at the bottom? Well, if you tipped it a little, it was easy to make it roll along halfway on its side. I just rolled it to the top of the stairs and let it go."

David nodded, "And then you ran back to bed—"

"And pretended to be asleep," Amanda said. "I'm very good at pretending to be asleep." She made a puckered, light-blinded face, like someone who had just been jarred awake.

"And the other time, when the picture was smashed?"

"I just threw that crystal thing at it and ran. It takes people a minute to wake up and get started moving no matter what wakes them up. I had my flashlight to see by, so I didn't have to stop to turn lights on and off. I'd only been back in bed about two seconds when Mom ran in. That was a close one."

"How about all the rocks?" David asked.

"Most of those were easy. I gathered them down in the creek bed and stored them in the loft of the garage. Then I'd carry them in my pockets until I needed them. Some of them I just left scattered around, and most of the flying ones I threw from the landing. From the landing you can get a clear shot at four different doors of downstairs rooms. Did you know that?"

"No," David said. "I guess I hadn't thought about it. At least not as a place to throw things from." He had thought about the landing as being a place where you could sit and tune in on the rest of the house. But what he'd felt was that the rest of the house was "in touch with" the landing—not "in range of."

"That time at the table—" Amanda went on, "the time the milk pitcher broke—"

"Yeah," David said, "I couldn't figure out how you did that one."

"I just brought a big rock to the table in my pocket, and then I got it ready in my lap and waited for something to distract everyone's attention away from me."

"Hey, I remember. The water heater was making noises."

Amanda nodded. "And when everyone looked at it, I just gave the rock a little toss up into the air and it came down right on the table. I really got that idea from you."

"From me?" David said.

"Sure. That time when you were doing the not-touching-metal ordeal. And you waited until everyone looked away and then you dumped your dinner in your lap."

A new idea occurred to David. "Hey," he said. "How about the seance? The rapping and everything. Was that—what I mean is— did you do that too?"

For a minute Amanda only looked at David through narrowed

eyes, but then she shrugged. "Yeah," she said. "I did it. I'll bet you'd never guess how."

"Well," David said. "I guess I haven't yet, anyway."

"With my toe," Amanda said.

"With your toe!"

"Uh-huh. I read about a poltergeist haunting that finally turned out to be a fake, only no one guessed for a long time. They found out these two girls had been doing it all—and they did the rapping noises with their toes. So, since I'd never really been a medium yet, and I wasn't sure I could do it, I planned the toe business just in case no real spirits showed up. So you kids wouldn't be disappointed."

"But how'd you make such a loud noise with just your toe?"

"Well, the book didn't tell exactly how the two girls did it, so I worked out a way of my own. I found a big heavy metal ring—something off a car engine—that just fit around my big toe. And I practiced till I could rap really hard with it. Then when I wanted to rap at the seance I just slipped my foot out of the slipper and rapped with the ring. It worked fine except my toe got swollen and I almost couldn't get it off. I had a sore toe for two days afterwards."

"Oh yeah," David said, remembering how Amanda had been limping around for a while. "But how about the thing in the closet."

"Oh that was easy. I made a red paper shade for the light bulb. You know how the light is in that closet—it's one of those old fashioned ones that hang down from a cord. Well, I tied a long string onto the chain that turns it on and I brought the string down under the Indian rug, so that it came out right under my chair.

Then I tied a button onto the end of it so I could get hold of it and pull it with my toes."

"But what about the head with the eyes?"

"I cut that out of cardboard and hung it on the inside of the curtain so that you couldn't see it till the light came on behind it."

"Wow!" David said. "Could I see how you did it?"

"Sure," Amanda said. "Right now?" She started to get up, looking almost the way Janie did when you admired something clever she'd done.

"Okay, in a minute. But there's another question I wanted to ask first."

"What?" Amanda said, sitting back down.

"Well, what I wanted to ask was—well, I guess it was—why? I mean, why did you do it?"

Amanda stared at the ground again. She glanced up at David several times before she said anything. The first time she looked up, David thought she was going to be angry, but by the next time she seemed to have changed her mind.

Finally she said, "I don't know. Not anymore. Part of the time I thought it was to get them to move out of this house because I didn't want to live way out here in the country and have to go to some crummy hick school with a lot of squares who'd probably hate a person like me. I thought if I scared everybody enough we'd have to move. But I guess that wasn't all the reason. I guess the most important reason was—to get even."

"To get even?" David asked. "What were you getting even for?"

"For everything. I was getting even with everybody for everything."

From the way Amanda said "everything" you could tell she thought she had a lot to get even for. After a while David asked, "Did you tell Molly about you being the poltergeist, I mean, up until last night? Is that what you were talking to her about?"

Amanda nodded. "Yes. I told her about that and a whole lot of other stuff. We must have talked about three or four hours."

"What did she say about all the things you did? What is she going to do about the smashed philodendron and everything?" David asked.

"I don't know. She doesn't either, at least, not yet. We didn't have time to decide anything much, but we found out a lot of things." Amanda leaned over and picked up a twig and began tracing patterns in the dusty ground. "I found out some things," she said.

"I know one thing I'd like to find out," David said. "I'd like to find out where that cupid's head came from."

Amanda looked at him quickly. "Me too," she said.

"Well, what do you think?" David asked. "Do you think it's the real poltergeist come back?"

"I don't know. Do you think so?"

"I don't know. You're the one who's supposed to know all about the supernatural and everything."

Amanda sighed and shook her head and kept shaking it for a long time. Finally she said, "I don't know. I just wish your dad were here. How long till he comes home?"

That really surprised David, because he thought he knew how Amanda felt about his dad. And he never would have guessed that even an army of poltergeists would make her glad to see Dad come home. He was about to say so when the back door opened and Janie came out with the twins right behind her.

David gave Amanda a significant look to remind her that the kids didn't know about last night and weren't supposed to find out. Amanda nodded, but at the same time she gave David a cold look that said she didn't need advice from him. Then she put her chin on her knees and sank into a gloomy silence.

Not knowing anything about all the trouble and worry of the night before, the kids were full of their usual early morning energy and enthusiasm. In fact they seemed to be more full of enthusiasm than usual. They bounced around the back porch, giggling and chattering and trying to get attention. They even began to get on David's nerves, and considering the frame of mind Amanda seemed to be in, he was sure they were getting on hers. When Esther got behind Amanda on the stairs and started to climb on her back for another piggyback ride, David winced, waiting for Amanda to explode and start yelling.

To his surprise, instead of yelling, Amanda took hold of Esther's legs to hold her on and galloped off across the yard, with Esther giggling and squealing on her back and Janie and Blair running along behind.

That really surprised David, and he was even more surprised that afternoon when he walked into his room and found Blair sitting in the middle of the floor playing with Amanda's crow. Blair was feeding the crow little bits of cookie. David noticed the crow's cage was sitting open on the window seat.

"Hey," David said, "does Amanda know you have Rolor in here?"

"Amanda knows," Blair said. "Amanda gave him to me."

David was positive that that was what Blair said, but he found it hard to believe.

"Are you sure?" he asked.

"Sure," Blair said. "And she gave the bumpy lizard to Janie and Tesser."

"Wow."

"The snake is for you."

"Wow," David said again.

He sat down on the floor by Blair and took a piece of cookie to see if the crow would eat out of his hand, too. The crow turned his head and looked suspiciously at David with one round yellow eye, but after a while he hopped closer and accepted the food.

David was helping Blair move Rolor's cage to a better place on the table in the corner when he noticed a big purple bruise on Blair's leg just below the knee.

"Hey, how'd you do that?" he asked.

"I did that, too," Blair said. "And that, too." He showed David another bruise on his ankle and a smaller one on his elbow. "The stairs did it," Blair said. "When I fell down with the box." He tipped his head to one side and looked thoughtful for a moment before he said, "Where is that box, David? Did you see that box?"

David was beginning to get an excited feeling. "Box?" he said. "What box, Blair? Was it a wooden box with a cupid's head and a bunch of rocks in it?"

Blair nodded. "Last night," he said. "The box fell down the stairs with me. But it's gone now. Did you see that box, David?"

Chapter Twenty

It took a lot of time and patience and dozens of questions before David finally got the whole story. As soon as he began to understand what Blair was talking about, he got very excited and impatient. And Blair always got more silent than usual the minute you got impatient with him.

Blair had almost quit trying to say anything, when he suddenly got up and ran to the window seat. David was starting to yell at him to come back and start talking, when he realized that Blair was trying to show him something. The window seat was where Blair kept all his toys, and David couldn't see what it could have to do with what they were talking about—until he looked inside. The back wall of the window seat had come loose and was leaning forward on top of Blair's toys, and behind it there was a dark and dusty hole. The hole was several inches wide, reaching from where the back wall of the window seat had been to the outer wall of the house. It was empty except for a lot of musty smelling dust. David remembered that smell from the night before.

"Is this where you found it? he asked. "Is this where you found the box with the cupid's head?"

It all began to come clear. Blair hadn't been sleepy last night because of his long nap, and after Amanda put him to bed he had gotten up and played with his toys. And somehow he had bumped the inside wall of the window seat and knocked it loose. And that was when he found the box.

"And you started down the stairs with it and fell?" David asked, and Blair agreed, nodding hard. "And then what? Where did you go then? You weren't there when we came to see what happened."

"I was scared," Blair said. "My leg hurt and somebody was yelling and I hid in my bed and waited for you. And you didn't come. And then it was morning."

So that explained it. Amanda's screaming had frightened Blair, and he'd gone back to bed. And he'd stayed there until he went to sleep. As soon as David had it all figured out, his first thought was to tell everybody. Amanda first, and then Molly and everybody. He's actually started out the door when Blair called him back.

"What is it?" he asked impatiently. "I'm in a hurry."

"Could I see it," Blair said. "Could I see the box?"

"The box isn't here," David said. "Ingrid put it somewhere but—" All of a sudden David remembered about the cupid's head, and he went over to his dresser and took it out. He sat down by Blair, and they looked at it together.

The head was just like the other ones on the banisters, except that under the coating of dust its wooden cheeks and curls looked a little shinier and less worn. Just like the other cupids, it had fat round cheeks and a small smiling mouth. At the bottom of the head, where it had been cut off, the wood was rough and jagged and unfinished, not smoothed down and varnished like the neck from which it had come.

Holding the head in his hands, David began to think about how it might have been cut off—and who had done it. And who had hidden it in the box behind the window seat wall, more than seventy years before. He supposed it was the poltergeist who had hid it—the famous Westerly poltergeist—and that only left one mystery. Had the famous Westerly poltergeist been a real ghost or had it only been the two Westerly sisters pretending to be one, in order to scare people—or get even—or something.

Sitting there, holding the cupid's head, David began to realize that he was feeling a little disappointed. Disappointed that there might not ever have been a real poltergeist. He knew, too, that the kids would feel the same way. And it was funny, but he didn't think that, at this point, Amanda would be the least bit disappointed. It seemed strange that Amanda, who was so crazy about such things, didn't seem to like the supernatural nearly so much when it really started happening. And the kids, who didn't know a thing about the occult world, seemed, on the whole, to enjoy it.

David let Blair play with the head, while he stretched out on the floor and did some serious thinking. Amanda had certainly changed since she started thinking there was a real poltergeist around. Would she change back if she knew there hadn't really been one? David wondered about that for a while and about some other things, and by the time he got up, he'd completely changed his mind about what he was going to do. He explained about the poltergeist and Amanda to Blair very carefully.

"Look, Blair," he said finally. "Let's not tell Amanda or anybody about your finding the box and falling down stairs with it. Let's not tell anybody anything about it at all. At least for a while. Maybe someday we'll tell them all about it. But first I want to wait a while. Okay?"

"Okay," Blair said. His smile almost turned into a laugh, and he jumped up and down a little. "Okay, let's don't."

David wondered if Blair was so pleased because he liked having a secret with just David, or because he liked not having to do all that talking and explaining. Or maybe it was because he had the same kind of feeling that David was having, about it being better to let Amanda go on believing in the poltergeist for a while. If that was it, it was amazing because David wasn't too sure he understood the feeling himself. But there was no use asking Blair what he was thinking—and besides, with Blair, thinking didn't seem to have a whole lot to do with understanding, anyway.

So David and Blair kept quiet and things went on about the same around the Westerly house. Amanda spent a lot of time with the kids or with Molly, and, after a day or two, Ingrid got tired of trying to solve the mystery and went back to the city.

Then, late in August, David's dad came back from the mountains. He came home tired and dirty and very glad to see everyone. And everyone was very glad to see him. Of course, they all told him about the poltergeist and what it had done, and of course he had to hear about Amanda and what she had done, too. In fact, Dad and Amanda had a long private talk about it not long after he came home. David never could get Amanda to tell him what they'd said to each other, but it must not have been too bad—because afterwards Amanda began to talk to Dad a little, even in public.

The only thing that Dad didn't find out was that Blair had been the one who had found the box and dumped it down the stairs. David couldn't tell him that, because he'd be sure to tell Molly and Molly would tell Amanda, and David still felt it wasn't time for her to know. Not yet.

So Dad had to go on wondering about that, along with everybody else, except David and Blair. Everyone talked about it and wondered about it, but Amanda seemed to wonder about it more than anybody. But not too long after Dad came home, Amanda stopped having to have somebody go with her everytime she went upstairs after dark. And as time went by and nothing else strange happened, she seemed to be wondering less and less.

Then one day something happened that made David, himself, start to wonder again. Dad had been home for nearly a week and the excitement had settled down enough so that David could do some things he'd been planning. One of those things was to put the long missing head back on the cupid. It took him most of one morning to get ready.

First, he had to sand the varnish off the neck edge, and then he filed and sanded the head edge down to match. Then he borrowed some very strong furniture glue from Molly. He was sitting on the landing smearing the glue on both surfaces, when Blair started down the stairs. He was carrying David's basketball.

"Hey, where are you going with that?" David said.

"Outside," Blair said. "To play. Okay?"

"Well, okay," David said. "Just be sure to bring it back when you're through."

But Blair didn't go on down the stairs right away. As soon as he noticed what David was doing, he sat down on the landing to watch. David was blowing on the glue to make it hurry up and get tacky.

After a while Blair said, "She'll like that."

"Who? The cupid? It's supposed to be a he."

"No. Not the cupid. The girl who told me."

"The girl who told you what?"

"To get the head out. She told me where to look. She wanted the cupid to have it back. I think she did."

David stopped blowing on the head. "What are you talking about, Blair? What girl told you where the head was?" He was getting so excited that he was almost yelling and, of course, that was a mistake. Blair began to get his worried silent look.

"That girl—" he got out finally, "—who lived here."

"You mean a girl who used to live here a long time ago?"

Blair nodded.

"You mean a ghost girl?" David was trying not to, but he was shrieking a little.

After a long time Blair nodded again, very slowly. "I think," he said. Just then the basketball dropped out of his hands and rolled down the stairs, and Blair went after it.

David started to run after him, but when he stood up he found that he'd absentmindedly put the cupid's head down in his lap. By the time he got it unstuck from his pants, Blair was out the front door. David frantically stuck the head onto the cupid and ran outdoors and around the house. He finally found Blair bouncing the ball in the driveway. But Blair absolutely refused to talk about it anymore. When David asked him, he only said he didn't remember.

Blair went right on not remembering, so David had to go on wondering. He went on wondering about it for a long time, particularly every time he went up the stairs and looked at that cupid with its head on—a little bit crooked.

Turn the page
for your first glimpse of

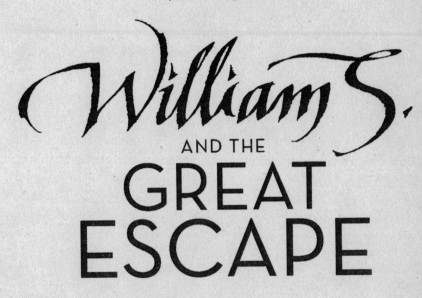

William S.

AND THE

GREAT
ESCAPE

by Zilpha Keatley Snyder

H is birth certificate, if he even had one, probably just said Willy Baggett, but for most of the seventh grade he'd been signing his school papers William S. Baggett.

William S. Baggett

But that, too, would change as soon as he made his move. No more Baggett then—and good riddance.

Actually, he'd started thinking about running away almost seven years ago. That was when he'd started going to school and began to learn, among other things, that not everybody behaved like Baggetts. And not very long after that he began putting every penny he could get his hands on into what he thought of as his Getaway Fund. Well, not quite every penny. He did spend a dime, now and then, on a Saturday matinee at the Roxie Theater. Watching how your favorite movie actors could make you believe they were all those different people was one thing he'd never been able to do without.

In spite of an occasional movie, his secret stash had grown pretty fast while the Baggetts still lived in the city, where there were lots of lawns to mow and flower gardens to water and weed. And even after they had to get out of town, he'd managed to add a few coins now and then by doing odd jobs at school—carrying stuff for teachers, and mopping up on rainy days for Mr. Jenkins, the janitor.

He'd made other plans and preparations too. Besides saving his earnings, he began to keep a long, narrow knapsack beside his bed, and all his most important belongings right there within arm's reach, ready to push into it. And then, someday, he would take his Getaway Fund out of its supersecret, hard-to-reach hiding place, sling his knapsack over his shoulder, and simply walk away. And that would be that.

But what then? Where would he run to? Over the years he'd changed his mind a lot, but just recently he'd come up with some interesting possibilities. Like, how about Hollywood? Or Broadway in New York City? Or even better, Stratford-upon-Avon. Okay, not likely. But, "We are such stuff as dreams are made on." Right?

He never told anyone, of course. Not even Jancy, at least not until after she'd pretty much guessed. But the little bit Jancy knew didn't worry him that much. His sister would never do anything to ruin his future career. He was sure of that. Well, he *had* been sure anyway, until the day her guinea pig got flushed down the toilet, which not only messed up the plumbing, but apparently changed everything.

Sweetie Pie had been Jancy's pet ever since her fourth-grade teacher got tired of a health class experiment that involved feeding some guinea pigs fruits and vegetables, and some others nothing but candy and cookies. Sweetie Pie had been one of the stunted sweet-stuff pigs, and she never quite made it to normal guinea pig size. Not even after Jancy went to the trouble to clear off a stretch of cluttered, weed-grown land to plant a vegetable garden. She did manage to grow a little bit of healthy stuff for Sweetie Pie, and she would have grown a lot more if Gary and the twins hadn't decided to use her garden plot as one end of their football field.

Even though Sweetie Pie never got much bigger, she was, according to Jancy, the smartest, cutest guinea pig that ever lived. But then came the first of August, 1938, and Sweetie Pie's story came to a sad end.

William found out about it soon after it happened, when he overheard the twins snickering outside the bathroom door. What he heard them saying was how they'd managed to "get rid of that stinkin' rat, and let Buddy take the rap."

William wanted to pound on the door and yell at them—not that that would have accomplished anything, except getting himself beaten to a pulp. Besides being extra big for fourteen-year-olds, Al and Andy were extra vicious. So William bit his lip and went looking for Jancy.

For a while he couldn't find her anywhere. Not in the room she shared with Trixie and Buddy, and not anywhere else in the big old wreck of a house. Not hiding behind any of the junkyard furniture in what might once have been a pretty nice living room, or out on the halfway collapsed veranda, either. But then, as he was checking the back hall, there she was, walking toward her room with her mop of hair hiding her face as usual. But when she saw him, she put her finger in her ear—their secret signal that asked for a talk in their private hideout.

Okay, fine. No amount of talk was going to do poor Sweetie Pie any good at that point, but William knew how Jancy must be feeling, and if talking would help, he was ready to listen. Ready and willing, even though it meant making a feverish (hay feverish, that is) trip to the barn—the huge, saggy, roofed building that sat about fifty yards from the condemned farmhouse where the Baggetts had been hanging out ever since they got more or less kicked out of downtown Crownfield.

Nowadays the barn was a kind of junkyard where all the Baggetts who were old enough to drive—not to mention the ones who drove even though they weren't old enough—had stashed the body parts of a whole lot of dead hot rods, pickup trucks, and motorcycles. Down there on the ground floor the scene was nothing but rusty carcasses, but up above the car cemetery there was a secret place that nobody seemed to know about except William and Jancy. A deserted area that must have been a hayloft back in the days when the huge old building had been a cow barn instead of a car dump.

So a moldy hayloft had become their favorite place to have a really private conversation, in spite of what it always did to William's hay fever. He didn't mind that much about the hay fever thing. Being forced to choose between being teased and tormented or having hay fever wasn't nearly the worst thing about being at the bottom of the Baggett pecking order.

On the plus side, the loft was fairly handy. All it took was a well-timed scamper across the cluttered yard to the barn door. And then a careful zigzag around and over fractured fenders and rusty radiators until you got to a narrow ladder that led up to a place where you could scrunch down behind a big pile of moldy hay and be fairly sure none of the bigger Baggetts would show up.

Up behind the haystack, in between William's sneezing and sniffing fits, he and Jancy had now and then managed to come up with the kind of plans that were necessary in order to survive as comparatively small and defenseless Baggetts. Plans like how to discourage Gary from throwing your books off the bus on the way to school, or where to hide your most precious possessions where Al and Andy couldn't get at them. So it was up there in the hayloft that William was waiting when Jancy's curly head and red, weepy eyes appeared over the edge of the loft floor.

The weepy eyes were no surprise. But what he certainly hadn't foreseen was how the conversation began. The very first words out of Jancy's mouth were, "Look here, William, I know you're getting ready to run away. You are, aren't you?"

Puzzled, William shrugged. "Well, yeah, I guess so. Sooner or later. Why?"

He was still wondering what his plans for the future had to do with the sad fate of Sweetie Pie, when Jancy cleared that up by explaining that she had decided that what happened to Sweetie Pie was the last straw.

"I'm just plain finished with being a Baggett," she told William fiercely. "So I'm going to run away too, as soon as ever I can."

William was shocked. "What are you talking about?" he

said. "You're only eleven years old. A little kid like you can't just take off all by yourself."

Jancy threw up her hands. "Listen to me, William," she said. "I didn't mean all by myself. I said *too*. Like, with you. And it has to be real soon. Like maybe tomorrow. Don't you get it?"

William got it, but he didn't like it. However, he knew from experience that when Jancy really made her mind up about certain kinds of things that was pretty much it—not much use to argue. But he kept trying.

"But the problem is," he insisted, "I'm not ready yet. Look at me, Jancy. I'm just a kid." He shrugged and screwed up his face in the kind of lopsided smile that an actor uses to show he's joking—mostly joking, anyway. "Well okay, a supersmart and talented person, maybe, but still just a twelve-year-old kid." He was kidding, but not entirely. He was pretty smart, all right. No Baggett, not even the ones who put him down as a smart aleck and teacher's pet, could deny that.

And as for talented? Well, according to Miss Scott . . . But that was another story. The only story he had to come up with right now was one that would keep Jancy from running away. At least for a few more years.

"The kind of help you'd need for a successful getaway," he told her, "is somebody with a lot more than just smarts. Like, what you're going to need is some big, musclebound type guy."

Trying for a laugh—Jancy usually liked comedy—he stuck out his skinny chest and flexed invisible muscles.

No laugh. Jancy listened, squinty eyed and silent. He

sighed. Even though she'd known about his running-away plan for a long time, she also knew, or should have, that he'd always seen it as something that was going to happen in the fairly distant future. And now, suddenly, it was like *right this minute?*

Things were moving way too fast. It wasn't more than an hour since the Sweetie Pie tragedy, and now Jancy was jumping the gun by announcing that she'd never been cut out to be a Baggett, and she was going to prove it by running away.

"Okay. Running away to where?" William asked. "Where you planning to go?"

Jancy raised her head and jutted her small pointed chin. "To Gold Beach," she said firmly. "I'm going to go to Gold Beach to live with our aunt Fiona."

William shook his head doubtfully. "I wouldn't count on it," he said. Fiona Hardison, their mother's sister, was a schoolteacher who lived in a little town on the northern California coast. A woman whom William and Jancy had met only once, right after their mother died, and that was four long years ago. "What makes you think Aunt Fiona would let you live with her?" William asked.

"Oh, she will," Jancy said. "She'll be so happy to get Trixie and Buddy back, she'll be glad to have you and me, too."

And that was how Jancy finally got around to mentioning an important minor detail. Not only would William and Jancy be running away together—they were going to be taking Trixie and Buddy with them.

Under the circumstances, Jancy's decision to give up on being a Baggett wasn't all that surprising. After all, she'd probably loved poor old Sweetie Pie more than any Baggett, except possibly William himself—and the two little kids, of course.

That was another thing about Jancy. She'd liked little things, the littler the better. Not that William, who was actually a year and a half older and a couple of inches taller than she was, could play that role very well. He wasn't really little, but according to popular opinion (Baggett opinion anyway), pretty much of a wimp. So maybe that's what made the difference with Jancy. William was aware that little and cute was way out ahead where Jancy was concerned, but skinny and wimpy might come in a close second.

That day in the hayloft, William's arguments got even more frantic after Jancy mentioned that her escape plan included Trixie and Buddy. "Holy Toledo, Jancy," he said, when she let that minor detail slip out. "You can't be serious. And I'll tell you right now that I am *very* serious about not helping commit a double kidnapping. You know what they do to kidnappers when they catch them. Like that guy who stole the Lindbergh baby. Zap!" He did an exaggerated quivering, stiff-limbed impression of an electric chair victim. Still no smile. He shrugged. "Anyway, I mean it. Count me out."

"But you told me——," Jancy was beginning when he interrupted.

"Okay, so I did say I was going to clear out, and I meant it. But I meant later. Like when I'm practically an adult. Like fourteen or fifteen. Not now, when I won't even be thirteen till next month. And as for you getting those two little kids all the way to Gold Beach? No way. Doing it all by yourself? I mean, look at you."

She did, and William did too. There she was, barely eleven years old, and small for her age. And at the moment—it was a blazing hot day—wearing one of Babe's outgrown sundresses. On Babe, who was fifteen, the dress had looked—well, kind of sexy, in a not very classy way. But on Jancy's skinny little stick of a body, it only made her look like the wrong end of a hard winter.

With the hay fever kicking in pretty badly, William had to stop to sneeze several times before he went on. "So I'm supposed to believe that what I'm looking at right this minute is a dangerous kidnapper who's going to nab two little kids and get them all the way to Gold Beach without getting caught? More than a hundred miles from here? And even if you managed to get that far before the police caught up with you, what makes you think Aunt Fiona would let you stay? She didn't even answer the last time you wrote to her."

"I know," Jancy said. "But she did write me two letters that were all about how awful bad she felt when Big Ed took

Buddy and Trixie away. Like how she'd had them and loved them for two years and would have kept them forever if Big Ed hadn't showed up all of a sudden to take them back."

"Yeah, I *know*," William said. "I remember." What he knew, and would never forget, was that right after Buddy was born, their mother, Laura Hardison Baggett, died. Died very suddenly, leaving behind newborn Buddy and two-year-old Trixie to be taken care of by Big Ed and a bunch of Baggett teenagers. William had been eight years old at the time, and he remembered that final scene all too well. Especially when he was trying not to.

Back then Big Ed had been glad to let Aunt Fiona take Buddy and Trixie away to live with her. Let them go probably because there was no longer any Baggett left alive who was willing and able to change diapers. William had been willing to try, and he'd said so, but nobody would listen to him. So the two youngest Baggetts went to live with their mother's sister, who kept them for two years before Big Ed decided to take them back.

That happened right after he'd married Gertie, his third wife. What Big Ed told the welfare people was that he took the two little kids back because Gertie wanted to be a mother to them. As far as William could see, Gertie wasn't, and never had been, the least bit interested in being a mother to anyone. The way William figured, it was a lot more likely that President Roosevelt's new welfare plan had something to do with Big Ed's decision to have all his kids under the same roof. The New Deal plan that gave really poor families a certain amount of money for each of their children.

"Aunt Fiona probably didn't answer your letter," William told Jancy, "because she was sure that if she got them back, Big Ed would just show up and grab them away again."

"I know." Jancy hung her head so that a bunch of her thick, streaky-blond hair swung down, hiding her small face. Jancy got teased about her hair—got called Mop Head and Rabbit Tail and even worse names. Actually, William thought her curly hair was her best feature, at least when it was clean and combed, which wasn't all that often. He'd told her so before, but now he said nothing at all, and after a while she said, "I know" again, in a faint weepy voice. "But I am leaving, for absolute sure and certain, and I just can't leave the poor little things here all alone."

"Humph!" William snorted. "All alone? Not hardly. Even with you gone, and maybe me too, that still leaves—let's see." He pretended to count on his fingers. "Seven"—he stopped to sneeze—"that leaves eight big Baggetts, if you count Gertie."

"Yeah, exactly," Jancy said. "That's exactly why I can't leave Trixie and Buddy here."

William got her point, and he couldn't help but agree, but just then another thought hit him. "I don't get it. What I don't get is why you'd *want* to bother with them. Well, Trixie maybe." He could sort of understand that. Trixie was kind of hard to resist. "But Buddy? I mean, wasn't he the one who flushed the toilet?"

Her face still hidden by her hair, Jancy nodded. "I know," she kind of gasped. And when she went on, her voice sounded wobbly. "But it wasn't his fault. Not really. Al, or else it was Andy—Buddy never can tell them apart—told him that a toilet is just the right size for a guinea pig bathtub, and when you flush, it's just like a guinea pig washing machine. It was that crummy twin's fault. I know it was awful dumb of Buddy to believe him, but he's only four years old. And who's going to tell him what else to not believe after both of us leave?"

William could tell she was crying by the sound of her voice, even though a heavy hunk of hair was hiding her face. "Crying won't do any good," he said.

But of course it did. After a few minutes of listening to her sobs and watching her skinny little shoulders shaking and quivering, he sighed and said, "Okay, okay. I'll think about it." And he meant it, even though it didn't take much thought to figure out that one reason, even the main reason, that Jancy wanted him to run away too was because she knew about—

"Oh thank you, thank you, William." Jancy interrupted his suspicious musings. And then her special talent for mind reading—at least where William was concerned—kicked in. "And it's not either because of your money," she said. "All that money in your running-away piggy bank."

William's snort was even louder. "My Getaway Fund is *not* in a piggy bank," he said.

"Well, whatever you keep it in," Jancy said quickly. "It's not because of your money. It's because you don't belong here either. You're not like the rest of them. You're not nearly as mean, and ever so much smarter and . . ."

William didn't have to listen to know the rest of what Jancy had to say. He'd heard her say it before when she wanted to get something out of him. But he also felt pretty sure that she said it because she knew it was true—at least the part about being smarter. But he still had a strong suspicion that his running-away money had a lot to do with it.

He shrugged. "Well, okay then, maybe I'm in. So what are your plans? I mean like *when*——and *how?*"

"When?" Jancy's smile, still tear wet, was wide and beaming. "Well, as soon as ever I can. Tomorrow or else the next day, for sure." She nodded again, so hard her curly mop bounced up and down. "Not a minute later."

"Ookaaay," William drawled the word out slowly. "But then comes *how*. How are you going to do it?"

"Well," Jancy's big eyes rolled thoughtfully. "I guess I'll just . . ." Her voice trailed off to a whisper and then came slowly back. "Well, I'll just pack up all their clothes"——long pause——"and something to eat on the way, and then . . ."

"Yeah," William prompted. "And then?"

Jancy's bony little face widened into a wobbly smile. "And then you'll decide what to do. You will, won't you, William?"

William shoved to the back of his mind a lot of troublesome unanswered questions concerning such things as *how* and *when*, and the even more serious one about what Aunt Fiona's reaction might be to their unannounced arrival. He sneezed again, wiped his nose on his sleeve, sighed, and said, "Yeah. Well, sort of looks like I'll have to."

Read all the NEWBERY MEDAL Winners from Atheneum!

THE HIGHER
POWER OF
LUCKY
by Susan Patron

KIRA-KIRA
by Cynthia Kadohata

lis Reynolds

'S SONG
nthia Voigt

DICEY'S SONG

FROM THE
MIXED-UP FILES
OF MRS. BASIL E.
FRANKWEILER
by E. L. Konigsburg

THE VIEW FROM
SATURDAY
by E. L. Konigsburg

MRS. FRISBY
AND THE RATS
OF NIMH
by Robert C. O'Brien

THE SLAVE
DANCER
by Paula Fox

PUBLISHED BY SIMON & SCHUSTER